MATT PETERS

Lord of the Lock

Copyright © 2023 by Matt Peters

All rights reserved. No part of this publication may be reproduced, stored or transmitted in any form or by any means, electronic, mechanical, photocopying, recording, scanning, or otherwise without written permission from the publisher. It is illegal to copy this book, post it to a website, or distribute it by any other means without permission.

This novel is entirely a work of fiction. The names, characters and incidents portrayed in it are the work of the author's imagination. Any resemblance to actual persons, living or dead, events or localities is entirely coincidental.

Matt Peters asserts the moral right to be identified as the author of this work.

First edition

This book was professionally typeset on Reedsy. Find out more at reedsy.com

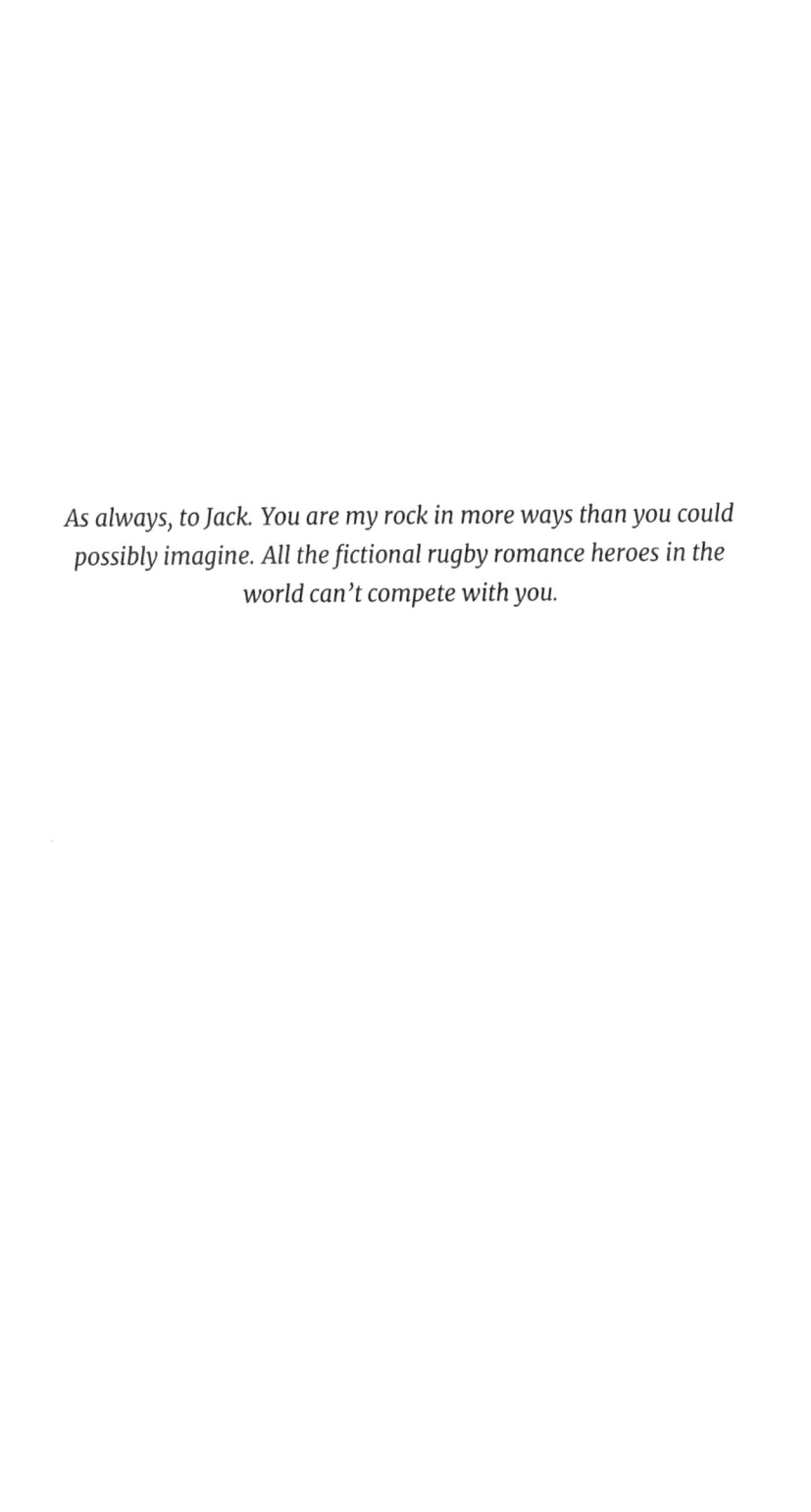

As always, to Jack. You are my rock in more ways than you could possibly imagine. All the fictional rugby romance heroes in the world can't compete with you.

Contents

1	Chapter One – Finn	1
2	Chapter Two – Nathan	9
3	Chapter Three – Finn	20
4	Chapter Four – Nathan	28
5	Chapter Five – Finn	38
6	Chapter Six – Nathan	43
7	Chapter Seven – Nathan	47
8	Chapter Eight – Finn	55
9	Chapter Nine – Nathan	62
10	Chapter Ten – Nathan	65
11	Chapter Eleven – Finn	71
12	Chapter Twelve – Nathan	76
13	Chapter Thirteen – Nathan	86
14	Chapter Fourteen – Finn	92
15	Chapter Fifteen – Nathan	104
16	Chapter Sixteen – Finn	116
17	Chapter Seventeen – Finn	126
18	Chapter Eighteen – Nathan	131
19	Chapter Nineteen – Finn	142
20	Chapter Twenty – Nathan	148
21	Chapter Twenty-One – Finn	155
22	Chapter Twenty-Two – Nathan	159
23	Chapter Twenty-Three – Finn	164
24	Chapter Twenty-Four – Nathan	174

25	Chapter Twenty-Five - Finn	184
	Other Books by Matt Peters	193

1

Chapter One - Finn

You're pathetic. My own internal voice was stronger almost than my external one. I'd always been a king in my own little domain, joker extraordinaire and centre of attention. I used my larger than life personality to mask the pain inside. I had partied hard, fucked relentlessly, and completely screwed up my whole life in the process. And rock bottom was where I'd ended up.

Rock bottom in this case was the small Welsh village of Pontycae, known as *Pont* unaffectionately by locals and visitors alike. Not that there were many visitors to Pont. It was a shithole, after all. It was where I'd chosen to start my self-exile after a couple of embarrassing missteps that had trashed my reputation in the world of rugby.

When I'd exiled myself I imagined that a quick call to the coach of my old team, Cardiff Old Navy, would have me reinstated and back on the payroll. But Garrett had moved on to coaching Wales and the new coach wasn't exactly keen to give up a place on his starting squad to someone with a reputation for derailing away trips and getting embarrassingly drunk at every opportunity. Not exactly star athlete material.

I gathered up bottles from the living room and passed through the kitchen to throw them into the rubbish bin outside. I had opened all the windows and the back door so that I could cover up the smell of alcohol that seemed to permeate everywhere. My best friends were coming round to check on me. I was determined that they see I was doing better. Even if I wasn't, exactly.

I sprayed a generous amount of Febreze around the room and made sure the little sofa was tidied up and tables wiped down. Now that the house didn't look like a homeless squat inhabited by angry alcoholics, it wasn't so bad.

At exactly 1pm there was a knock at the door, and I headed to open it with my heart in my mouth. Outside was a grinning Rhys Prince and his ridiculously well-styled Daddy of a boyfriend, Callum.

"How goes the day, Mr Anderson?" I asked as the big Scotsman pulled me in for a hug. Callum was one of the few people on a rugby field who almost looked eye-to eye with me. But I was still a couple inches taller than him. "Have you gained some weight?"

"Well not all of us are international rugby players any more," he said, ruffling Rhys' hair and then seeming to realise what he'd said. "Shit, I didn't mean...you'll be back to playing in no time."

"Sure," I snorted a laugh back, but his words had cut deep. If I hadn't been such an idiot then I would never have lost everything I held dear in life. But I was washed up at the age of twenty-seven, and I had no idea how I'd dig myself out of the hole I was in.

"How's my favourite star?" I asked, grabbing Rhys and pulling him in for a bone-crushing hug to diffuse the tension

CHAPTER ONE - FINN

in the room. "Score any tries against Scotland recently?"

"Enough," Rhys smirked, nudging Callum in the ribs.

"My nationalist heart lies with Scotland but my dick likes it when Wales win, what can I say," said Callum. "When Wales lose, I have to get the tissues out for an entirely different reason."

We all laughed, and it felt for a second like all the tension really had gone out of the room. We were just three old friends having a laugh, not two of the biggest legends in the game of rugby coming up to the arse-end of nowhere to console their washed up friend.

"Come on in," I said to the two of them, gesturing them into the living room. Not much had changed from when my grandparents had lived in the valley - the decor was still old-fashioned enough to be considered antique, and the sofa was a squishy floral thing that I had never actually ascertained if my grandmother had died sitting in. Now she was six feet under and my parents were living hundreds of miles away, I had no desire to find out.

"Tea? Coffee?" I asked. The only big changes anywhere in the house were all the fancy electronics I'd brought from Cardiff. In the living room I had my top of the range games consoles and TV, and the kitchen was decked out with my smart-fridge, smart-washer and smart....well, everything really. All my appliances were connected to one another and to the internet in some way, which had been great in Cardiff where the WiFi was speedy. Here, things crashed more often than not.

"Alexa, three shots of espresso," I said. Thankfully, there was no delay and the coffee machine started to hum as it ground down the beans.

"We should get one of those," said Rhys as I brought the

coffees in. "They're well cool."

"Around my kids? They'd be ordering more than I could afford as soon as they figured out how to use the thing," Callum laughed.

"Tell them their Uncle Finn misses them," I said. I had a soft spot for Logan and Olivia. They were sweet kids and Callum was nice enough to let me around them when lots of people were wary of my influence because of my past stupidity. I did my best not to be too bad an influence on them.

"They miss their Uncle Finn too," said Callum. "How's living back up here? Any good local pubs?"

"Callum," Rhys warned in the least subtle tone I'd ever heard.

"Seriously Rhys, you don't have to walk on eggshells around me. I can go for the odd pint without being a complete loon," I lied. As far as he knew, I was getting a real handle on any alcohol dependencies. So long as he didn't hear my bins rattling with the sound of bottles everything was fine.

"Well in that case, fancy going out for a meal?" he asked. I groaned internally. I *could* do it.

"Go on then, let's find a pub in this shithole," I said.

***

The Eagle was rough, but they did a good burger. At least that's how I justified it as Rhys and Callum followed me in and Rhys' eyes widened at the sight. The old place hadn't been updated since about 1973 and the tables were never as clean as they could be. Despite it being only 1pm, there were a couple of local alcoholics in the corner already off their face on Special Brew and who knew what else.

CHAPTER ONE - FINN

"Morning," one said to me with a little too much familiarity, and I nodded briefly before dragging Rhys and Callum over to a table in the corner.

"Stop staring like you're on a foreign excursion," I said to Rhys. "This isn't the third world."

"Sorry, I just..."

"Surely you've played rugby in some rough places?" I asked.

Callum chuckled. "I remember when I was amateur and we played a match in Glasgow that ended after ten minutes because of player fighting. I think I lost a tooth that day. That was *rough*, but it was fun."

I remembered then that Rhys, despite only being a couple years younger than me and almost a decade younger than his boyfriend, hadn't come up through the amateur ranks in the same Valleys shitholes that I had, or the places in Scotland that likely looked very similar to where we were sat.

"I'll get you both a drink. Pint?" I asked. "Don't look at me like that, Rhys. I can have a pint and not relapse."

Never mind that the relapse had already happened. I headed to the bar and ordered three pints off the grizzled old bartender who had been behind the bar back when my friends and I had started drinking at thirteen.

I brought our pints over and set them down in front of Rhys and Callum. "What's on the menu, then?" Rhys asked.

"Burgers," I replied. He really was too precious for this place.

"What kind of burgers? I love burger places."

I pointed to the scrawled whiteboard at the back of the bar. "Well you can have a burger, or a cheeseburger. If you ask nicely you might even get some sauce."

"Oh." Rhys looked back down at his pint and his cheeks turned red. There was a pub down the road that offered nicer fare, but it was always packed out as the only decent place in town to get a meal. Every date night, wedding party, and birthday took place at the Pont Hotel down the road.

Callum slipped his arm around Rhys, unconcerned at where we were, and kissed him on the top of his head. "Seems that rugby being a man's sport died back when I was making my way up through the ranks, eh. All on silver platters now..."

"Piss off," Rhys replied. "One of us has retired to nice, warm, comfy commentary boxes, and one of us still gets down and dirty in the mud. I wonder if you can figure out who..."

I laughed along with them both and looked around the pub again. The place never changed, and neither did the people. Which is why I was so taken aback when a shock of hot-pink hair entered the room.

The bright pink was attached to a little man, surely at least a foot shorter than me and skinny. He was dressed in matching denim shirt and jeans and was wearing too-big round glasses. He was frowning as his eyes darted around the room, like a herbivore checking a field for predators before darting across. He held the door open for an older man in a wheelchair I vaguely recognised and then they both headed to a table in the very far corner of the room, ages away from anyone else.

"Hello, Earth to Finn?" Rhys waved a hand in front of my face and brought me back to our table. "Something caught your eye?" he smirked.

"Nothing," I muttered. "Anyway. Burger. Cheese. Sauce?"

"I'll get these," said Callum, standing up. "I know what you both like." He walked over to the bar with his empty pint glass to order.

"And I know you like a twink," Rhys muttered. "Do you and that guy know each other?"

CHAPTER ONE - FINN

I looked over to where the guy was stood at the bar. Something in my mind was firing up at the sight of him, but I had no idea if it was recognition, arousal or both. I knew most people in this town, so it was weird that I couldn't quite place him. Especially with his bright pink hair.

He was ordering at the bar but even then his eyes were darting around the room like he was scared of something. He seemed to instinctively lean away from Callum and his bulk, and he walked quickly back to his table as soon as he'd been served his pint and a glass of water.

"Bloody hell Finn, stop looking and answer my bloody question," Rhys said.

What question? Oh, yeah. "I don't know him," I said. "Though I really should..."

"Thought you were swearing off hookups whilst you were here?"

"I am, I just mean...everyone knows everyone around here. And there's only one high school in the village, so I'm sure I should know him...he might be familiar..."

"Bloody hell, £1 a burger," Callum interrupted. "And £3 a pint! We should come here more often."

"We really should *not*," Rhys said, and I had to agree with him. It was nice to have the two of them around, but it messed with my ability to wallow in peace. A tiny little part of me wanted to be around the table with the old alcoholics and to drink myself into a stupor. Instead I forced myself to drink my pint at a glacial pace as Callum finished off a second and third and Rhys had a second. I had to prove to them I was in some kind of control.

The door to the pub opened and I heard the familiar laughter and voices of a couple of the lads from the local grassroots rugby team. Like most people around here, they had grown up in the town and had gone to the same high school, joined a rugby team and worked in similar trades. I forgot their names, as they'd played for Pandy rugby team whilst I'd played for the semi-professional Pont. Those of us who were lucky enough had gotten out in the end, gone on to bigger and better things. Maybe I was even unluckier for having come back.

Both their voices stopped abruptly and I looked up. I thought they might have spotted the three international rugby stars in their midst. But they weren't looking at us at all. They were looking at the pink-haired man in the corner. And his fear looked like it had been ratcheted up to a whole new level.

The second they took a step towards him, I was up on my feet and ready to fight.

2

Chapter Two - Nathan

My father was late. Again. And in the month I'd been home, it was getting increasingly hard not to go stir crazy with his constant antics and cries for attention. "Come on, you wanted to go out!" I shouted down the hallway of my parents' new bungalow.

"Well give me a minute, I can't work with this bloody thing!" My father bumped into the door frame with his wheelchair as if to prove a point, even though the door frames had been specifically widened to help him. I knew I should feel sorry for him but...after a month of him battering me and my mother down, it was starting to grate on my nerves.

"The nurses offered you lessons, you just chose not to take them up on it," I muttered. "And you swore at the prosthetics team..."

"I was confused, I was under anaesthesia!" he lied.

"Sure." It was exhausting arguing with him. Which is probably why my mother had given up so easily. "Right, so are we heading to the hotel for a drink like you wanted?"

"I don't want to go to the *hotel*. I want to go to the Eagle."

"Then you can go by yourself, Dad."

"It's not accessible, I can't get the door open by myself."

"Then ask someone to help you."

"I should never have raised such an ungrateful son." And there it was, he'd won the argument with one simple, horrible sentence. Every potential retort died on my lips.

"Fine, let's fucking go," I muttered. As my father left the door, he *accidentally* ran over my foot with one wheel. There was no apology, nor would I expect one. I locked up the door and followed him as he pressed forward on the little nub that propelled the electric wheelchair over bumpy pavements and toward our destination. One of the places I dreaded the most.

We didn't talk on the journey over, which gave me a lot of time to think on my fear. And to let it grow. There were four establishments in all of Pont to gather and have a drink. There was the Pont Hotel, run by my parents until the smoking had taken my father's leg. Mum ran it now, mostly by herself with constant nagging from him and an ever-growing list of happy customers. Then there were the rugby clubs, owned and run by Pont and Pandy rugby clubs themselves. Pont were a semi-pro rugby team who had sent a couple of players in their time over to the Welsh squad. Pandy were amateur players, and the source of most of my fear for coming home.

The Eagle was a kind of truce ground where both rugby teams frequented. I hated the place, and the way those players had treated me way back was the reason I'd scarpered years ago, firstly to Cardiff and then to the tiny town of Hiraeth on the West Wales coast. But my father's illness had brought me home to Pontycae. To Hell.

The Eagle was quiet, but that was nothing unusual in the

CHAPTER TWO - NATHAN

daytime. I kept an eye out for people I knew as I opened the door for my father, and my eyes briefly alighted on the three big men in the corner. I recognised a rugby-player build when I saw one but I vaguely recognised the three men too. I wasn't about to go prodding, in case they were tormentors I'd somehow forgotten.

As soon as I stood to walk to the bar, one of the men stood upon and walked over. *Of course* that would be just my luck. But as soon as he opened his mouth, I knew he wasn't a harm or a face from my past. "Three burgers please...and another two pints," he said in a deep, thick Scottish voice. All of the men that had bullied me had been Pontycae born and raised. The man gave me an easy smile as he gestured to me to be served next, and I did my best not to cringe away from him as I ordered mine and my father's drinks.

When I'd moved to Hiraeth, it was to totally remove myself from the drama and shit that followed me everywhere in Pont. Even then, it had taken some time to be comfortable around some of the taller, burlier men there, much as they reminded me of the Pandy rugby players. And then as soon as I'd settled in, my mother had called me. Dad's operation had gone fine, she had said, but he desperately needed help around the house. Help she couldn't give when she was running the Pont Hotel from dawn to dusk. So I'd come home, and so far avoided places like this. Like the Eagle.

As I got back to the table, I looked over at the table of three again. Of the three, the one I thought I recognised locked eyes with me again. He was massive, easily six and a half foot tall and built with arms that could crush a car, and had deep brown eyes that I could melt into from across a room. His dark hair was cropped close to his skull and there was stubble playing around the edges of his cheeks. Once he saw me looking, his eyes dipped and a blush darkened his tanned cheeks. I recognised him still, but there was no malice in his eyes. And I was pretty sure I had my bullies memorised to the last detail. It was strange to see so gentle a face on a body like his.

My father and I drank in silence, him sipping on a dark ale and me a lemonade. I had no desire to talk to him, and for once the alcohol seemed to soothe the constant pain that he told us he was in. I felt sorry for him sometimes - Type 1 diabetes wasn't his fault - but the refusal to help himself, his cruelty to my mother, his nurses and a complete mental block on going to therapy and his complete attitude change to all of us around him were all enough to make me angry. He was making life horrible for all of us, and he had turned my life back upside down. I was looking around corners again and scared to leave the house. Because of him. And...well, the other *him*. Lewis.

As soon as my father was done with his pint, I took a note from his wallet to get him another. If drinking bought me his silence for now, I would keep him drinking until the bar closed.

I stood up, and at the same time the door creaked open. And there were voices. And if anything proved my own hypothesis about remembering my bullies, it was those two voices that sent a shiver of anxiety from my head to my toes. I turned from the table to look at them, and their voices died instantly as they spotted me. My own fault for having a hair colour that could be seen from space.

Ryan and Charlie were long-time players for Pandy Rugby United, and they were inseparable best friends. And they were good friends with Lewis, the cause of all my problems. They were both above six-foot tall and people often had joked about them being twins back when I hung around with them. The biggest difference being that Ryan was wiry and muscular, whereas Charlie was built bigger, *like a brick shithouse* my dad would have said in a happier time.

They took a step toward me, and I took a step backward, bumping up against the table. I had no doubt that they wouldn't care about beating the crap out of me in a place like this.

"You know we've told you not to come back here," said Ryan. His knuckles cracked ominously under one palm.

"After what you did to Lewis, I'm surprised you didn't leave the fucking country," said the other.

I held my hands up even as I cowered away from the two of them, desperate to show them I was no harm to them. Out of the corner of my eye, I was aware of the man from the other table approaching, and I knew then that I must have somehow forgotten the worst bully of them all. Because he was massive, and he dwarfed the two of them in both height and stature. His arms could rip tree-trunks out of the ground and those fists were scarred like they'd seen a hundred fights. If he was on their side, I worried that one rogue punch could kill me

"P-please," I stuttered. "I-I-I'll leave. No need t-to fight."

I had practically flattened myself up against the table, my father remaining curiously quiet behind me as the three men approached. And then the giant slipped around the other two. So he wanted to get the first punch in. Figures. My breaths were coming out faster and faster but I balled up my hands into fists. I might be terrified, I may not be able to make the man budge an inch, but I was going to put up a real fight. I expected that he would snap all five-foot seven of me in half with one swipe.

And then one of his massive hands scooped me up from the table into an embrace, crushing me against his side and holding me up on shaking legs. "Weenie-beanie!" he said to me. "I've missed you so much. I can't believe you didn't tell me you were back in town."

I didn't need to imagine my own expression - I could see the shock mirrored in Ryan and Charlie's faces. If the man wasn't holding me up with one of those massive arms I'd have collapsed completely to the floor.

"C'mon, love — why don't I introduce you to some of my best friends." He gestured over to the table where the other two men were now stood and looked prepared to fight if they needed to. Ryan and Charlie blanched from the forehead down. They might have stood a chance against this man together, but not the three of them. "You can catch up with your local friends later, alright?"

Both men took a step back, and then edged over to the bar. They weren't leaving, so I allowed myself to be shepherded over to the table by the giant. "Dark ale, was it?" he said over his shoulder to my father. I heard a grunt, which was the closest we'd get to conversation from him.

The giant deposited me in one of the bench seats opposite the two other men. One was a young, gorgeous twunk of a guy with blond hair and deep blue eyes. The other was the tall ginger Scotsman I'd seen at the bar. None of us spoke for a second, and my heart skipped a beat as the giant squeezed into the booth next to me and pushed a small shot glass in my direction. "For the shock, dear," he said casually.

I couldn't help but lean away from him and the other two. These were the kind of people who'd made my life a living hell. "Don't drink, fine, I'll have it," said the giant. He took the shot and downed it like it was nothing.

The blond across the table rolled his eyes. "I'm Rhys and this is my better half, Callum." He gestured to himself and the strawberry blonde Scotsman on one side of the table. His voice had just a hint of a Cardiff accent, but he was otherwise very well spoken. "And this big *coc oen* of a man is Finn." He gestured to the giant at my side, who grinned down happily at me, seemingly oblivious to my discomfort.

"Coc oen?" asked Callum.

"Lamb's cock. Weird Welsh insult," said Rhys with a grin. "I'll go get you some water..." he waited patiently.

"Nathan," I said when I finally realised what he was waiting for.

"Nathan. I'll go get you some water."

Finn looked around conspiratorially and leaned in to whisper. "I got your dad that dark ale. Didn't seem too pleased with me, but I'd rather you not sat over in that corner next to those two twats."

He pointed over to where Charlie and Ryan were sat, just a few feet from my father. For some reason he glared at me rather than at the two men who had threatened his only son.

"He's not pleased at much," I muttered despite the still-present fear.

"So why don't those two twats like you?" Finn asked loudly enough to be heard by the whole bar. I shrunk down in my seat, desperate to be anywhere else. But Charlie and Ryan didn't make a move, so it was obvious they were still intimidated. Rhys came back to the table with the water and passed it over to me.

"Long story," I muttered quietly. "I don't really want to get into it right now."

"Well they need to know to keep their hands off my boyfriend, because I will beat the shit out of anyone who touches him!" he was practically shouting by now, but it seemed to have the desired effect. Both men stood and left the bar immediately, leaving behind the remains of their drinks. Finn's wide grin never left his face. He had an extraordinarily lovely smile for someone so terrifying and big.

"Real smooth, Finn," said Rhys.

"Boyfriend?" Callum asked with a sly grin and then a wink at me. My heart was running at a million miles an hour. Last time I'd been a rugby player's boyfriend...well, that's why I was in the horrible situation I was in.

"I had to think quickly, my Bonnie Scottish friend," said Finn. "I could have taken both those fuckers down if I wanted to but I have a reputation to rebuild, and knocking out the grassroots of Welsh rugby would not have helped me very much at all."

I laughed and my fear started to dissipate just a little bit. The two men across the table seemed nice overall and Finn harmless. Those arms could do some serious damage, I still believed that, but not to me.

"So you guys...play rugby?" I asked.

All three exchanged a look and laughed. "Rhys is currently one of the best players in the world, Callum retired from rugby a legend of the game and I..." Finn hesitated for a second. "...I'm just taking a little break from the Welsh squad." His smile had been replaced by a downturn in his mouth and a little furrow in his brow.

"You're joking," I said, looking round at them. I tended to avoid Wales' national sport after all the bad experiences I'd had with it. But if these guys were international rugby players... "what the hell are you doing here?"

"I live here, I'm from here," said Finn. "Started as a player for Pont, got scouted for Cardiff and then for Wales. And then..." he tailed off. "...and then I decided to come home for a bit."

CHAPTER TWO - NATHAN

There was more to that story than he was letting on. But I wasn't going to pry. I'd let him keep his secrets, and he would let me keep mine. In theory. All he would have to do is talk to any of the Pandy boys and he would have the whole bloody story, embellished with details from the other side.

"Nathan!" called my dad from the corner. He held up his empty pint. "We're leaving."

I rolled my eyes and stood up. Finn stood aside for me. "Thanks...for your help," I said. I turned to the other two, now fully aware of their status as international rugby stars. "And...thanks for your service?" I said, feeling stupid as soon as the words escaped my lips.

"Two secs," Finn said to the other two, placing a hand on my shoulder and following me and Dad from the pub. Finn looked around outside before letting go of me. "Just wanted to check they weren't waiting around to jump you," he said.

"Thank you so much. It really means a lot," I said.

"Come on, Nathan. I'm going to need help getting over the pavement by the house and I'm getting cold," my father whined.

"Duty calls," I said to Finn. I found it easier to give him a genuine smile.

"See you around, Weenie-Beanie," he said.

* * *

Later that night, I was safely tucked up in bed and finally letting myself unwind. My father had made life difficult for Mum as soon as she got home, and I was exhausted from mediating between the two and trying to stop mum from doing absolutely everything for him.

My curiosity got the better of me, with Finn's earlier shadiness piquing every bit of interest I had in him.

So I opened up a tab on my phone and googled *Finn Wales rugby*, just to see what had made him decide to put International Rugby aside and retire to this shithole when he still looked in his prime. The first thing to pop up was a full-page spread of his coming out article, as well as his full name, Finn Roberts - so that's where I recognised him from - as well as pictures linking him with Rhys Prince and Callum Anderson's relationship, which had started oh-so-romantically with a kiss on the rugby field.

I clicked backward out of the link. Rhys was still playing, and Callum commentating, so why had Finn given up? What had pushed him to leave rugby? And then at the bottom of the search results, a tiny line of writing informed me I would need to change my security settings to 'off' to access all of the results. I clicked it.

And the results changed completely. *FINN ROBERTS ON HIS KNEES* was the first link that came up, linking to a site that looked halfway between news and porn. When I clicked it, I realised that the whole site was dedicated to celebrity nudes. With some trepidation, morbid curiosity and a splash of guilt, I pressed play.

The video was graphic, and had Finn on his knees in a forest, light from a torch blinding white on his face as he...as he sucked someone off, their moans barely audible over wind and crackling of leaves under Finn's knees.

A sick, perverse part of me liked seeing Finn in that way, but I shut off the video before it could go any further and put my phone down. The poor guy had given up the world for that? I knew what it was like to be chased away because of something that wasn't my fault. My heart ached for him.

I didn't get much sleep that night.

3

Chapter Three - Finn

For the second day in a row I was pretending to be someone I was not. I had put on an act for my friends, put on an act to save a guy from being beaten up, and now I was putting on an act to get a job and save myself from complete boredom.

The first part of that act was a suit. I'd worn the tailored suit many times after Wales matches. Rugby players weren't paid half as much as football players, but during the Six Nations we were paid a £20,000 bonus for a full-game appearance. So I'd bought myself a lovely suit with the proceeds after one, just to make myself look important and expensive.

I pulled on a watch that cost ten times the suit. I'd always struggled with analogue, and I didn't even check to see if it was still keeping time. It was all about looking good.

I looked at myself in the mirror and laughed, without much humour to it. There was a half-empty beer bottle by my bed and tissues from a wank I hadn't cleaned up. It was a miracle I could fucking fool anyone into thinking I was competent or I'd turned over a new leaf. I was a mess, a sad, sorry mess. But if I pasted on the old Finn Roberts charm for just a couple of

CHAPTER THREE - FINN

minutes then maybe I would have something to get out of bed for in the morning.

A flash of pink seemed to shine in front of my eyes for a second, and I rolled my eyes at myself before turning away. Little twinks with hot pink hair would not — *could not* — be the reason I got up in the morning. No matter how precious they looked or how much I wanted to make sure they were safe. Despite falling back into old habits with laziness and alcohol, I'd been off sex completely since the video that had ruined my life. I was not about to let someone derail me so publicly again. And the thought of having sex had given me the ick ever since, anyway. I didn't want a repeat of what had happened before.

Until... I'd helped a guy in terror escape some good old fashioned bullies. And as he steadily relaxed and got used to me, even despite being obviously scared of me for some reason, I had wanted to pull him close and tell him everything was going to be OK.

And Finn Roberts didn't do that. I did not think sensible thoughts about men or women. My brain and cock had always directed me to sex first, emotions later. And once the sex was done, they gave up on the idea of emotions and bailed the fuck out of there.

But with Nathan...he seemed sweet, and kind, and I couldn't imagine what someone like him could have done to deserve the treatment he'd gotten from the Pandy rugby players.

My mind had still drifted to sex later on, when I was alone with my thoughts and a bottle of beer. And I'd finished into a tissue to the vision of that bright pink hair on pale skin, and those deep grey eyes looking up at me. *Pathetic.*

I looked down at my Rolex. Nope, I still couldn't tell the time on the thing. So I took my phone out instead and looked at the big, obvious numbers on the home screen. 9am. It was time to go.

My grandparents' old house was just over the road from Pont's ground. It was how I'd fallen in love with rugby. I crossed over the road and slipped through the turnstiles on one side of the stands. One side of the pitch was dominated by a big corrugated aluminium stand, one tier with space for about 3000. Around the edges of the pitch was more uncovered seating across a couple of rows, probably enough to seat a thousand more. It was small-fry compared to the Arms Park, but this place was where I'd fallen in love with watching rugby, and later, playing it, before making my way into Cardiff and Wales' ranks. This place was where I'd learned to live and breathe the sport.

Coming back didn't feel so special.

It was the off-season, and it was quiet. With players only paid part-time wages for semi-pro clubs and often having full-time jobs or school during the day, it would always be quiet in the daytime. I walked past the pitch to the squat redbrick building over in one corner of the grounds. It hadn't changed in twenty years.

I knocked on the locked metal door and something...no... someone else who hadn't changed for twenty-odd years greeted me. Rhod Nolan had coached Pont for over thirty years and in that time he'd just gotten a bit older, with obvious wrinkles all over his face and hair that had turned completely grey. Otherwise, he was wearing the same eighties tracksuit that he'd been wearing when he first scouted me twenty years before.

"Finn!" He held out a hand for me to shake and then pulled me in for a backslapping hug. "Glad to see you around. Come in, come in!"

CHAPTER THREE - FINN

I felt suddenly very stupid in my expensive suit and fancy Rolex. I might have needed them for an actual interview, but to be interviewed by Rhod? He'd much more have appreciated if I turned up in training gear and started doing push-ups.

Once we were in the building I looked around. *Wow.* Some things had changed. Inside, the old bare-bones equipment had been replaced by new state of the art treadmills, weights and rowing machines, and the electrics were LED, not flickery old lights that rarely worked like when I'd last trained. "Nice set up you've got here," I said.

"You'd know all about that if you bothered showing up every once in a while," Rhod said before flashing me a smile. "Why don't we do the interview in here instead of my office? I spilled coffee in there in the pre-season and I haven't been able to get the smell out."

I laughed and took a seat he offered on a rowing machine, feeling even more stupid in my fancy clothes.

"I'll be honest, I was surprised when I saw your name on an application for a coach," he said. "I knew you were taking a break from rugby but..."

When he didn't carry on, I picked up the thread he'd left. "But I need something new for now, Rhod. And you know I love grassroots rugby."

"*Loved*," the old man corrected. "I haven't seen you around here since you got the call-up to Cardiff. You haven't exactly shown loyalty to old Pontycae since you left."

"Can you blame me?" I asked before I could stop myself.

Rhod's bushy grey eyebrows, once ginger, drew together. "Yes, I can. Hate where you came from all you like. But I don't expect my players to pull the ladder up after them. If you were good enough for professional rugby, any of these boys could have been. And you never came back to inspire them."

"Sorry, Rhod."

"Well, you should be." But then he smiled. "We will not turn our backs on you, however. You've got the job. I'm still manager, I've been around too long to give that up easy. But we need a coach who can keep up with the lads. And ladies, now. That's a new one. Women playing rugby...wonders never cease."

I breathed a sigh of — relief, maybe? I still hadn't figured out my emotions after all the crap that had come before — but maybe this was what I needed.

"I looked up interview techniques online and everything," I muttered.

"C'mon, one of Wales' best applying for a job with Pont? It was always going to you. Though it helps that you can probably afford us paying you a pittance." Rhod stood up and clapped me on the shoulder. "I did have one concern about employing you, and old Bill sorted me right out."

"Jenkins?" I asked, remembering a heavy-drinking old man from my days as a player. "What was the problem?"

"I worried with your....with the nickname and rumours that were going round about you."

My heart chilled. "Rhod, if there's any kind of homophobia I'm out. You know they're not just rumours, I'm bisexual and I thought we were working to cut that shit out of rugby."

Rhod raised one eyebrow. "I know, lad. I meant *the Horse*."

I snorted, I couldn't help it. "You were worried about my big dick? And how did old Bill Jenkins convince you it wasn't big?"

"Stop being a smart-arse or you're not getting the bloody job. When you were here last, you were one of our best players. But you weren't everyone's friend on this team. If you could seduce someone's girlfriend, you would. That, and I saw you kissing a boy under the stands after a match when you were seventeen. So no, your bisexuality has never bothered me. You riding roughshod over other players to get a quick bang is what bothers me, and I'm not having you do it as a member of coaching staff. Some of the boys whose ladies you took last time are still playing. But from the sounds of things, I don't need to worry about that any more."

"And why is that?" I asked.

"Bill saw you with some pink haired boy in the Eagle last night. Says you're smitten."

"Ah, yes," I said. "That."

* * *

"Fuck, fuck, fuck." I felt like pulling my hair out as I paced my little living room. The first thing I'd wanted to do when I walked through the door was crack open a bottle of beer, but I'd resisted. I'd chatted with Rhod for a little bit longer about the demands of the job and the tiny perks that came from working part time for a mostly-amateur team in the arse-end of nowhere.

But Nathan remained a problem. My little ploy to save him had blown up into a lie in a town small enough that gossip flew around faster than light. And I didn't know how to fix that. Would Rhod care if I wasn't in a relationship with the guy? I thought so. Me being a bit of a shagger had caused enough problems when I was seventeen and playing for the team. I could see why something like that would concern him now when the papers had made sure that I had grown that reputation to a whole new level.

I tapped the button on my phone to have my coffee maker make two double shot espressos. This felt like either a drink myself stupid or four shot kind of problem. And if the espresso didn't work, I was sure there was some vodka in one of the kitchen cupboards. I could make espresso Martinis, kill two birds with one drink.

How could I possibly contact Nathan? What would I say? Would he be willing to say he was my boyfriend, keep up the ruse I'd started? What could I offer him in return? I paced toward the kitchen as the coffee machine beeped when there was a knock at the door.

For fuck's sake. The one thing I didn't need was visitors "What?" I asked loudly as I opened the door and almost ran into the wall of flowers in front of me.

"Take them, take them!" The flowers tilted forward and I grabbed them before they could fall on the floor, revealing bright pink hair and big tortoiseshell glasses.

"Nathan?" I asked.

"Oh thank God," he said. "This was the third house I'd checked. I'd be embarrassed if I had to knock on any more."

"And you knew my address....how, exactly?" I asked.

"Mum knows everyone who's ever lived in this village. I mentioned your name and she guessed you were living in your grandparents place. '*White house on Edward Street*,' she said. Just couldn't remember the number."

"And you brought flowers?"

"Yes...um...as a thank you for saving my arse in the pub. I'll go now."

Nathan took a step backward and I watched almost in slow motion as he fell backwards on the concrete step. My rugby reflexes took over. I threw the flowers into one hand and stepped forward to catch him with the other. He was light as a feather compared to the rugby blokes I'd had to keep stood up on the field. For a second, he recoiled from me like he was trying to get out of being saved. And then he managed to right himself with a little help, and took a tiny step back, still encircled in my one arm. Once I knew he wasn't about to fall over again, I let go.

"Guess I should get more flowers," he said with a shaky smile. "That's twice you've saved me from a concussion."

The espresso machine beeped again from the kitchen, like it was angry I'd forgotten the two cups waiting for me. "Coffee?" I asked him. "I...accidentally made two."

Nathan's eyes narrowed and he took a — much more careful — step back. "Why?"

"I have a proposition for you," I started, but the words had the opposite effect of what I was expecting. Nathan shook his head silently and walked off into the night.

4

Chapter Four - Nathan

My mum had been kind enough to let me have the box-sized spare room to sleep in and Dad's old office for business. Dad had complained for hours, but on this one thing Mum had stood firm. And I was thankful she had, because there was so much to do it was insane.

In shutting down my old shop in Hiraeth, I'd lost out on some face-to-face business from big fans of *Thrones of Blood* who congregated in the village to watch its filming and for conventions, but for the most part my business was online. Which is why I spent every minute my father wasn't demanding care holed up in the office keeping my business afloat by packing and sending online orders. The whole place was filled with nerdy memorabilia, and The Nerd Emporium had made a name for itself worldwide. I packed one *Doctor Who* order destined for Canada and pasted the label on it as I hummed the theme tune to myself.

The problem with working alone in one room was the amount of time it gave me to think. And when my thoughts were going along the lines they were, it was dangerous to give me time to

CHAPTER FOUR - NATHAN

think.

Stupid, stupid, stupid. I had spent so long controlling the automatic revulsion I had for bigger men in Hiraeth — and there were enough of them there — but being back in Pontycae had put me in a spin again, where people like Finn, who I could see had complete Golden Retriever Energy, were scary to me in the moment. I had no idea if he'd been inviting me in for just a coffee or for...more, but the fear of that in the moment had me running scared. Because he might want to take advantage. And there would be fuck all I could do about that if he did.

I heard the doorbell go off, and Mum answered it. Her voice was muffled as she spoke. Since my Dad had started being such a complete and utter twat, she didn't get as many visitors as she used to. It was nice when she did.

I heard steps creaking up the stairs. Heavy steps, alongside Mum's lighter ones. And then the bedroom door creaked open.

"Nathan, you've got a friend here to see you." Mum said casually, and I felt my heart ratchet up a notch and my breathing escalated. Had he finally come to see me, to warn me? Was Lewis about to walk through that door and drag me back to where I'd come from?

Instead, another giant walked through the door. A big friendly giant with a small bouquet of flowers. Finn smiled at me hesitantly, and I smiled back in exactly the same way. I wanted to curse God and thank him at the same time. Because Finn was a big, gorgeous goof who'd rescued me from some not so nice people. And my logical brain knew that. But my instincts didn't agree. Every time someone like him walked into a room in Pont, my instincts kicked into fight or flight. If I'd just met him a years ago...I'd have been instantly attracted to him. And he would've been a rugby player with a reputation for sleeping with anything that moved. So perhaps the universe was against me one way or another.

"I'll leave you to it," said Mum. She closed the door behind her and my heart rate kicked up a notch. I was locked in with him. I looked down at the package in my hands and controlled my breathing as I heard the springs in the sofa compress. I looked up, and Finn was sitting on the other end of the sofa, squeezing his massive body into the tiniest space imaginable.

"Sorry," I muttered. It was embarrassing that he'd caught on to my fear so easily.

"No worries, Nathan. People think I'm stupid, but...if there's something about me that freaks you out, I can keep my distance. I've worked out that much."

"Distance involves bringing flowers to my house?"

"Distance is...yeah, this is pretty stupid," Finn stood up.

"No, wait. Sorry. Sit down." I clipped out the words. I kept my eyes trained on the polythene packaging in my hand as I sealed it and pasted an address over the seam, then looked back up. Finn was now perched on the arm, at the very extreme of the room. As far as he could get from me.

"So, why the flowers?" I asked. "And how did you find out where I live? Wait, that first one is probably the important one."

"Same way you found me," said Finn. "Little village, ask where the guy with the hot pink hair and his dad with one leg live. Someone's bound to know."

"Ah. And..."

"The flowers? They're my apology. For saying you were my boyfriend the other day."

"But I brought you flowers," I said. "I was grateful for that."

"I know, but I forgot the one rule about living in such a little place..." said Finn. "People talk."

CHAPTER FOUR - NATHAN

I groaned. "Everyone knows everyone's business."

"Yup. And I applied for a job the other day, and part of the reason I got the job...was you putting me on the straight and narrow. Coach figured out I won't be fucking half the squad and their girlfriends if I had a steady boyfriend."

"Oh God, that's so embarrassing," I giggled. "So the flowers are an apology for..."

"For the fact that people are going to be talking about us...and for my next request."

My heart ratcheted up a notch again. Requests from men of Finn's size weren't always requests. Men who knew their size often knew how to use it.

"What do you want?" I asked, perhaps a little too harshly.

"Just...sorry, I know this is stupid. If...if anyone asks you about us, just say we are going out? It'll save my face with the coach, and then when I'm back in Cardiff in a couple of months it'll all be forgotten about. I'm not even asking for any dates or anything, just...pretend we have had them."

I wanted to laugh. "That's seriously all you want? Sure, whatever. I'll tell them we met on a dog walk up Caerphilly mountain."

"But I don't have a dog."

"Neither do I, but it's just as implausible as the rest of this."

"Why is it implausible?" Finn asked, a note of offence in his voice. "Because you're clever and I'm not? Because you've obviously got...whatever this is going on here, and I'm an almost unemployed bum?"

"No, Finn..." I didn't know what to say, so I changed tact as quickly as I could. "So if we're going to pretend to be together, we should know more about each other."

"So you'll do it? I haven't offered you anything in return!"

Finn said. He was smiling, like he still didn't realise how fucking insane this whole idea was.

"You don't need to offer me anything. Last night, on the walk back from your house, I walked past Charlie and Ryan. I thought they were going to...and then they crossed the road. They're so scared of you that they chose not to start a fight with me. And that is the best thing that's ever happened to me."

There was silence for a second. "I have to ask, Nathan. Why don't they like you? What was I saving you from?"

I hesitated. I didn't want to give too much away. Finn wasn't my therapist and he definitely wasn't my boyfriend. "A few years back I was in a relationship with one of the Pandy players..."

"There are gay guys playing for Pandy?"

I held up a finger to silence him, something I wouldn't usually be too confident in doing. But I needed to get my version of the truth out.

"Yes. At least, there was one. And it took him a little while, but he came out. And we were...we were something. But he wasn't always nice, and when I broke up with him, he told all of his mates horrible things, like that I'd been cheating on him. And I hadn't...in fact, he had, but you know rugby players. Loyal to the end. So I started getting threatened in the street. He'd turn up to my house begging for me to come back to him and every time things would get worse."

"Fuck, man. I'm sorry that happened to you." Finn pushed the flowers across the sofa to me like a dog offering its treat to another.

"Eh, I got the hell out of here and built up a life I liked, selling nerdy memorabilia for lots and lots of money. Collecting is *in* nowadays. If my Dad hadn't had such a drastic operation

I doubt I would have come back. But I'm facing my demons now," I lied. If Finn hadn't saved me at the Eagle I'd have about ten less teeth and would have run back to my safe place faster than my Dad could roll. My demons were facing me, and I was losing.

"Still, man. I'm sorry about what you've gone through."

"Maybe if I wasn't so little and pathetic I'd have been able to whoop their arses back years ago," I mused. I picked up a figurine from the pile and wrapped it in bubble-wrap.

"Well, I'm here for at least the next couple of months. In exchange for fake-boyfriend services, I offer real life bodyguard services," said Finn. I looked up at him as I laughed, and it was like I saw the moment that a lightbulb went off over his head. "Wait. What if I could help you with that second problem?"

"Got a stretching rack, have you? I'm five and a half foot of nothing."

"No, no. See, I'm not earning much in my job - it's three days a week in the evening, and that's fine. I *have* money," Finn said almost defiantly. "But as a benefit of my job I can book the training facilities when no one is using them. If you want to look that little bit more intimidating..."

"So you agree," I said. "I'm pretty pathetically built. Do you really think any muscle is going to help me stand up to the kind of blokes who's like to knock me out?" It was hard not to let the anger creep into my voice.

Finn sighed. "You're reading into this too much. See, when I was in school, I was nothing special. I was little, I had fuck-all when it came to brainpower or grades and I definitely wasn't getting any attention off boys or girls. I was spotty and I had braces because my teeth had grown out all weird. And when I was fourteen, I shot up in height. Mum used to say I was like a bean sprout. So then I was stupid, tall and gangly with acne. It was even worse than when I was small. I was noticeable once I'd grown. And when people made fun of my height, or my spots, or how I looked like a gust of wind would fucking knock me over, I felt pathetic."

I nodded. I knew that feeling. I'd been feeling it for a solid half of my life.

Finn continued. "So I did the one thing I could. I hit the gym. Exercise made me happier, and the guys who used the gym played for the school rugby team. Getting big helped me to feel a bit less of a target, yeah. But the real benefit was how I felt. Exercise makes me happy. Seeing that I've taken control of the one thing I could makes me happy. Eventually the braces came off and the acne faded. But I had still taken action to make myself feel better. And in doing that, I happened to make friends with some of the rugby lads who used the school gym at lunchtime. By the time I was sixteen I had finally found my tribe. And I was getting attention off the girls."

"So...you're not offering because you think I'm fucking puny?" I asked, finally feeling my cheeks pull up a little bit as I spoke.

"I'm offering because I think exercise gives people happiness, and you could do with a little bit of happiness. And a bit of muscle never hurt anyone...'til it punched them in the face."

"Fine then," I said, holding out my hand to him with more confidence than I felt. "So long as you're not expecting me to join the rugby team."

"And in return, you cover for me if anyone thinks I've gone all straight and narrow." Finn reached forwardly and gently clasped my hand in his much bigger one. "Fake boyfriends," he said with a smile.

CHAPTER FOUR - NATHAN

"Fake boyfriends," I agreed. "Less straight, if you make me less narrow."

Finn laughed quietly and then looked down at his hands. Now we'd negotiated, things felt awkward.

"So where did you go to school?" I asked when a second had gone without him speaking.

"Pont High, you?"

"Pont."

"I don't recognise you..." he said. "Are the glasses new?" I pointed up at the picture on the wall above him and he craned his neck to see. "Oh, P'raps not."

The picture in question was me at seventeen years old, in the second year of sixth form with my high school diploma and my big tortoiseshell glasses.

"Oh, I remember you now," said Finn. "A year below me, right? You were cute as hell."

"Thanks, but I was *not*,' I said. I had begged Mum at the time not to buy the picture but she refused. "If you'd told me I looked cute back then, I'd have thrown myself at you."

He pulled out his phone and showed me a picture. "Believe me, I was not about to ask you out in school. There's me in school, sixth form rugby championship."

"You are *joking!*" I said. With a wispy moustache and terrible mullet, the Finn of a decade ago, pictured running across the rugby field, somehow looked older than the man before me. "Who de-aged you?"

Finn picked up a TARDIS I'd been about to pack. "If I had one of these, I'd travel back in time and tell myself that the mullet was a fucking mistake. I looked like if David Hasselhoff and Hulk Hogan had a baby."

"Weirdly specific reference," I said, grabbing the TARDIS and stuffing it in the package with the cuddly Doctor Who monster toys. "Though this is my favourite show."

"Always been more of a *Thrones of Blood* man myself," said Finn. "They're the only books I've ever read."

"Really?"

"Never thought I was any good at school, but I picked up *Thrones of Blood* at some hookup's house when he was asleep and I couldn't find a key to get out...I was hooked man."

"Ever watched the TV show?" I asked slyly, pulling my phone from my pocket and prepared to blow his mind.

"Are you joking? I once faked an injury in a Cardiff game to watch the finale," he said. "That Daniel Ellison could *get it*."

"Well he's very loved up with his partner," I said. I found the photo of me, Danny and all my other friends from Hiraeth on my phone and showed it to him. "Jealous?"

"Fuck off, you have not met Daniel Ellison." Finn took the phone from my hand and zoomed in. "It's not a cardboard cut-out? He really is that good looking in person?"

"Yes, and a good friend of mine too."

"You're kidding. Keep this up and I just might have to make you my real boyfriend," Finn said.

I laughed, only because it was said in such earnest. It was easy to get along with Finn, despite my initial fear. He really was a puppy of a man in a Great Dane's body.

"Right, I need to get these orders packed. So if you're not going to help, you better shove off," I I said.

Finn smiled. "I'm off to work, anyway. Got to get my first day's prep done before training starts for the season next week." He fiddled with his phone for a second. "There we go, I've AirDropped you my contact details." My phone buzzed in my pocket. "I'll send you over details when I'm ready for your first training session."

Finn got up and left, and the little room felt bigger and emptier without his presence.

5

Chapter Five - Finn

I'd never had a classroom before. It was weird. But after watching one trying session with the boys, I knew they would need more visual help in defence before they had any chance of nailing it physically. I'd been going through defensive drills for an hour, but I wanted to show them all a bad defence in action.

I pointed at the projector screen. The lads, all between seventeen and thirty, were sat on exercise equipment around the gym. I'd selfishly put up a video of one of mine and Rhys' runs against his boyfriend. It was the best video to show the lads, *obviously*. It just happened to be one of me.

"So you'll see how Rhys passes to me just before Callum can impact him? The whole Scottish squad was focused on the smallest, fastest player. Rhys was so good that they forgot I existed. I'm not pretending this was a good tactic by any means from me and Rhys because it left us wide open to being tackled. But for just a second it was like the Edinburgh's defence evaporated, and that let us score. If you are defending you *cannot* let your guard down for a second, or this happens."

I pressed play. Rhys was all ahead of the pack, me trailing just behind. As Callum reached for Rhys, he passed to me. Callum slammed into Rhys on impact and I ran over the line to score a try. All because Edinburgh had been sloppy.

The camera zoomed in on Rhys and Callum, the moment after impact. As far as I knew, this was long before they were a thing. But in the moment, both of them were so completely wrapped up in each other that I wondered how the whole world hadn't seen they were in love. And then they both stood and Rhys looked like he was about to swing for Callum, and the good times were over.

"Every couple has arguments. Some are lucky enough to get to punch them out on the rugby field," I said. The lads laughed. I was glad to see a lot of the old bigotry from back in my playing days was gone. Plenty of the lads I'd fooled around with had wives and kids now, but the old overtones of shame had gone from the squad for the most part.

"My girlfriend plays for the women's team. I wouldn't want to fight her on the rugby field, she'd knock my spark out," said one of the younger boys. More laughter from the whole squad.

"Then you better be good to your lady," I replied. "Right, that's enough for this evening. Make sure you pick up your defensive drills from the pile on the way out, as well as my workout plan."

There were a few eye-rolls and groans as the lads filtered out from the room. Rhod was a great coach overall, but he was a bit old-fashioned in terms of in-between training sessions. I wanted the lads eating well and exercising between training.

The younger guy who'd mentioned his girlfriend hung back for a second. He was tall, almost as tall as me but so gangly that I guessed it must be recent. It was obvious he was young and growing into his frame from his clumsy gait and acne, but he was fast on the pitch from what I'd seen. "Finn, can I say something?"

"Sure…" I said, racking my brain for his name. But with thirty-odd members of the squad as well as the youth and women's teams it was tough to keep them all square.

"Ben," he offered.

"Sure, Ben."

"I just wanted to say…thank you for being you. I know coming out wasn't easy, but I'm bi. And it gave me confidence to tell my girlfriend when you came out."

"And she was OK with it?" I asked, concerned.

"She was great. I'm lucky to have her."

"Good lad." I patted Ben on the shoulder, and he lumbered out, knocking into the rowing machine on the way. Once the place was quiet, I started tidying the projector screen away and squaring up any training guides that hadn't been picked up. It had been two weeks since I'd seen Nathan and our first training session was imminent.

I checked my phone - nothing since he'd confirmed he was coming. I headed to the changing room to change out of my shirt and jeans into something more appropriate for training. I had a tank top and shorts in my locker, so I stripped down to my boxers to put them on. Before I could re-dress, a door creaked open behind me. When I turned around, Nathan was standing there, pink hair wind-ruffled and his glasses in one hand. He was wearing ratty tracksuit bottoms and a t-shirt that said *The Angels Have the Phone Box*. A blush had crept up his neck and was deepening across his cheeks.

His eyes roved over me just once before he took a step backward. "S-sorry," he said. Like a ghost, the door swung closed before I even noticed he had gone. I stepped into my shorts and grabbed the tank top, yanking it over my head as I followed him out onto the training floor.

Nathan was sat on one of the rowing machines, eyes downcast as I approached. As soon as he heard me, he looked up. "I really am sorry," he said. "I just...I didn't mean to walk in on you in there like that. I wasn't sure where you were and thought you might be cleaning up or something and I just..."

"Nathan, chill. I'm a rugby player. I've seen more men changing than I've had hot dinners." I noticed he hadn't brought a bag of spare clothes with him. "You know you're welcome to use all the facilities, right? If you're going to be getting all gross and sweaty here then you can always use the showers, sauna or ice bath afterwards. I've booked the whole place for myself two nights a week."

"Oh-OK, thanks," said Nathan. "I just...I don't want you thinking I was walking in on you to perv or anything. I'm not... I'm not like that."

I laughed. "That makes one of us. Gay, bisexual straight or even asexual, I can tell you now we've all had a little peek in the changing rooms. It's only natural. We all want to know how we measure up."

"Oh." Nathan's blush had returned in full force, but he stood up. "Shall we start?"

"Yessir, fake boyfriend." I led him over to the free weights. "Today we'll focus on upper body - your chest, arms, and stomach. I've booked out the place on Thursday too and it's your choice if you want to do leg day or cardio."

"That all sounds horrible," said Nathan with a smile. "You do this twice a week?"

"I do this every day," I laughed. "This is my favour to you, it's all up to you how you use me."

There was that bloody blush again, as Nathan and I realised the double entendre at the same time. "Filthy bastard," I said to him. "C'mon. Let's go." I wanted to see that blush again, it gave him fire. Made him look less timid and scared.

I put him through his paces from the start on bicep curls, reverse curls and then the various weight machines. I made sure to show him every machine and did my reps in his rest time. We'd hardly spoken since the last time we'd seen each other except to arrange the session, and it felt like we'd taken a step backwards, like he was more reserved again than the last time I'd seen him.

"It's not fair, you lifting triple what I do," he said at one point as I strained against a particularly heavy weight on the shoulder press.

"It's not about...*fuuuuck*....what you can lift straight away," I said, giving up on my set. "It's....about starting somewhere and doing your best to get fucking better at it."

"Yes captain," said Nathan.

I worked him until we were both pouring with sweat. There was something gorgeous about him as he pushed that bright pink hair away from his face, which was almost the same colour as his hair now from exertion.

"I...I'm done," he finally admitted, slumping down.

"I was waiting for you to admit it," I laughed. "Good work, soldier. Leg day Thursday?"

"I hate you...but yes." Nathan held out one hand and I shook it, both of us gross and sweaty. He gave me a tentative smile, and for the first time I felt like maybe contact with me wasn't freaking him out.

6

Chapter Six - Nathan

8 Years Ago

I hated PE in school. I didn't understand why they ever made us play rugby and tennis and football or any of that shit in the first place. Most of my friends were girls, and we were segregated in PE, so I had to spend the whole time with laddish, stupid and immature rugby boys whose whole personalities were centred around muscles and girls. I was eighteen years old, an adult, and the school were still forcing me to exercise when I didn't want to.

We had been running hurdles in the gym, which wasn't as bad as playing rugby outdoors, and I could compete with the rugby boys because I was thinner and lighter on my feet than most of them. It still left me a sweaty mess in the middle of the school day. We all trooped off to the changing rooms, most of them talking and bantering with one another, me taking the rear of the group by myself.

As always, I got changed in the corner with my eyes carefully downcast to avoid drawing the attention of any of the lads. Any excuse to call me a faggot was warranted in their eyes, and the fact I *had* to change with them didn't seem to cross their minds when they accused me of being in the changing rooms to watch them. I didn't shower with them for that reason, because to be naked in their presence — even if I thought most of them were ugly, smelly bastards — would be reason enough for them to say I was perving on them and they might beat the shit out of me.

So I changed out of my sweaty gym clothes quickly and into my uniform, almost bumping into a couple of the boys because I was so determined to keep my eyes downcast. I hated knowing that I'd smell vaguely of sweat and the gym all day.

I was almost to the lunch canteen when I realised I'd forgotten my phone in the changing room. It was a crap little flip phone but Mum would kill me if I'd left it behind. So I turned around and headed back, thankful that most if not all of the boys would be done in the rooms. I only hoped my phone hadn't already been taken by one of them.

I opened the changing room door quietly. I could hear the showers still running, so I crept over to the corner of the room and grabbed my phone. I pocketed it and walked toward the door when I heard a moan coming from the shower block. *Is someone hurt?* I thought.

I walked over to the shower block quietly. The whole place was shrouded in steam, and I could see a figure in the corner. "Is everything alright?" I asked, stepping on to the wet tiles and walking closer.

And then I saw what was happening. Lewis Jacobs, one of the school's top rugby players and all-round ladies man, was standing under the hot spray, back against the tiles and cock in hand. He was a gorgeous, muscular lad with round shoulders

CHAPTER SIX - NATHAN

and mousy brown hair that was being plastered to his head by the spray. He moaned loudly as he stroked himself fast and hard, evidently reaching the point of climax.

I was so focused on the action going on in his hand that when my eyes finally made their way up from his cock, up his toned stomach and wide pecs, I almost jumped when I noticed he was looking right into my eyes. He stared at me as he stroked himself to completion and spilled all over his hand and onto the tiled floor. He splashed his hand under the shower and within seconds all evidence was gone into the drain. And I still stood still, unable to move from the spot.

Lewis stepped out of the spray and toward me. Was he going to threaten me? Or just beat me where I stood? He was still at half mast as he pushed me up against the tiled wall opposite the showers, both hands on my shoulders. "Do you like what you see?" he asked. He was a good six inches taller than me and I had to look up at him as he pressed his whole body up against mine.

I couldn't move, couldn't think, didn't know what answer would spare me a beating. So when he dipped his head toward mine and kissed me, I had no idea what to do. I'd never been kissed by another boy before. Was this what always happened? His tongue explored my mouth and after a second I kissed him back. I could feel myself getting hard, straining against my trousers.

Lewis could obviously feel it too as he looked down and smirked. "I won't tell anyone about you deliberately finding me to perv in the showers, and you don't tell anyone about this, OK?"

I nodded, my whole body shaking in fear, anticipation and arousal."Good boy," he said. "Now piss off, I need to get changed."

  I rushed out of the room as fast as my feet could carry me, slipping on wet tile and having to grab onto a bench for support before I left the room. My shirt was wet and my dick was still half-hard as I emerged into the outside air, wondering what the hell had just gone on.

7

Chapter Seven - Nathan

"Dad, I've left you with your food in the fridge and your beers are on chill. Is there anything else you need from me?" I asked.

He was sat in the living room in his wheelchair, watching *Countdown* for what felt like the forty-seventh day in a row. "Wouldn't matter if I needed something else, you obviously have more important places to be. Stopped caring about your father pretty soon after coming here, didn't you?"

"Mum will be home in an hour, and you said you were fine with me going out when I mentioned it yesterday," I rebutted.

Logic didn't matter. My father just rolled his eyes and looked back to the TV. "Who is it you're going out with anyway?"

"I'm training with Finn. He's helping me get fit."

"And Finn is..." my father asked, still not taking his eyes from the TV. "Five, SMILE."

"Finn is..." I hesitated. Surely it couldn't hurt to spread the white lie exactly as we'd intended to. "Finn is my boyfriend. And there are two S's on the board. You're missing an easy six. SMILES."

"Typical." He tore his eyes from the TV again. "So that man

is your...boyfriend?" he asked. "How come we've never met him properly?"

"Because Mum works ridiculous hours, and you'll only leave the house to go to the Eagle," I said, not exactly lying. "Anyway, it's early days. I don't want to jinx things."

"Well don't mess up like you did with the last rugby player," he said.

That stung. That *really* stung. "Bye, then."

"GROPES, six letters," was the only reply.

I grabbed my bag from the hallway and left through the front door. My arms still hurt from the workout two days before, but the exercise with Finn had got my endorphins running. I had so many bad memories of PE in school, and so few happy memories of exercise, that it genuinely surprised me how good it could feel to get a sweat on.

I was nervous about Finn's insistence on showering afterwards, and the thought had brought back some less happy feelings from my school days and beyond, and all the crap that had caused me to want to leave Pont in the first place.

The mixture of feelings, good and bad, followed me all the way to Pont's ground. I didn't have as many reservations about this place as I did Pandy's. Pandy's had a whole other side to it that I'd be happy to never see again.

"You came back!" Finn shouted from across the gym as the door closed behind me.

"Didn't think I would?"

"I once had Rhys Prince, rugby star, on the ropes after a tough session and he said he never wanted to see me again. So you've got more staying power than the Welsh Prince of Rugby."

"What of Welsh rugby are you, then?" I joked as I got closer to Finn's massive frame. He was wearing a tank top with

CHAPTER SEVEN - NATHAN

deliberate ragged rips down the side which did very little to cover him up in any way, but if I had a body like his I wouldn't be covering up either. He wasn't as ripped as I'd expect from all the exercise, I knew that from accidentally walking in on him in the changing rooms — but he had broad shoulders, arms that could crush boulders and thighs and calves that wouldn't be out of place in a watermelon-crushing ASMR TikTok video.

"I'd be the...clown of Welsh rugby, I guess," Finn said. "I just want to see people smile. And I fucking clowned my way out of a career too. Oh well. Shit happens. Oh, and they used to call me Lord of the Lock. Because I'm fantastic in the air."

He smiled then, but it didn't crinkle the sides of his eyes like I'd seen them do before. I understood then how people talked about smiles that didn't reach the eyes.

"What's the order of the day then?"

"Well, I'm going to make you wish you were never born," replied Finn with a devilish smile. Something like that might have made me run for the hills before. But Finn was the first valleys rugby player I'd ever met that made me feel more safe than intimidated. The fact that he could turn any sadness into a joke, or that his innuendos seemed more equal-opportunity than predatory, just drew me in.

He turned to an intimidating looking machine and laid down on it before bunching his legs up to press against a plate. I could see he'd set the scales at 250kg and started pushing his legs outward. "The one thing you don't want to do..." he started, sweat beading as he pushed his legs forward and back, "is lock your legs. That could hurt. So just bring your knees back to your chest, and push forward until they're almost straight, but not quite. OK?" He jumped off the machine and gestured for me to get on. He was smiling, but his legs were already shaking.

I nodded, and got into the seated position with my legs up like he had. I pushed hard, temples popping, and couldn't move the plate an inch.

"Whoops, let me just..." Finn moved the pin upward. "Let's try 80kg, ten reps, and we can move on up to see if we hit your limit."

With a little strain, I got ten reps done. And after Finn had another go with his colossal weight I managed another ten on with an extra ten kilograms of weight. Finally, I strained my way through 100kg, sweat beading up on my forehead even faster than it had on arm day.

"Well done!" Finn held his arm up for a high five and I had to jump to reach it. What followed was less fun — as it turned out, leg day could be very, *very* punishing. But an hour later as we finished a 'gentle' ten minute walk on a stair machine, with my legs like jelly, I was glad I'd done it. Because my body felt energised, my mind clear.

"Good job today, mate." Finn stepped forward for a hug and I took a step backward to avoid him. Much as he was feeling like a safe space, there was something that still made me feel uncomfortable in a situation where I couldn't escape.

Finn, as always, was completely unaware of my panic, and he just sniffed at his armpit instead. "Oh yeah, good call. No hugs 'til we've showered, ey. And no hugs in the shower. You might be my fake boyfriend but I don't want you trying it on!"

He laughed and walked over towards the changing rooms, yanking his vest off before he'd even gotten to the door. I steeled myself for a second before following. School had left me with some stupid insecurities, but I could do it. I could face up to a shower with a man who so far hadn't judged me at all.

When I stepped into the changing rooms, the shower was

CHAPTER SEVEN - NATHAN

already running and the shower block was filled with steam. Despite the modern facilities everywhere else, the shower block was the old fashioned open kind with no cubicles or privacy. I could see Finn in one corner through the steam, and as far as I could see he was facing away from me. I took my glasses off which blurred things just a little bit more, and stripped before I could change my mind.

I headed over to the opposite shower-head from Finn and turned it on, yelping out loud as the water came out freezing cold. Finn laughed from the opposite corner, but I didn't turn to look at him.

"We used to have about a minute of warm water between us," he said. I dipped my hand under the water and stepped under as it turned warm. "Imagine twenty teenagers cramming themselves into this shower block just to catch the bit of warm water before it was cold enough to make our junk shrivel."

"I'd rather not," I shot back. "Never liked PE in school. Too many straight boys thought I was looking at them." There, I'd said out loud, not in so many words, what had caused this stupid fear of showering in public.

Finn chuckled. "Do you have shampoo over there?"

I shook my head, and a bottle of shampoo slid across the floor and knocked the side of my foot. So he'd been looking over at me.

"I never had that problem," Finn said. "No-one was accusing me of looking at them."

"Why, because you weren't out?"

"Because they were looking at me," he said.

I picked up the shampoo and squeezed some into my hand before rubbing it through my hair, over my armpits and in other more sensitive areas. The water was lovely to be underneath

51

now it had warmed up, but I was still resolutely staring at the tiled wall. Even if Finn had taken a peek, I was still too scared to look elsewhere. I was more scared of looking at him and seeing his eyes on me, which was completely irrational from the other side of a steamy room when I didn't even have my glasses on and wouldn't know at all if he was looking. But still, I faced the wall and washed the shampoo off me.

And then I realised what he'd said. "Wait, they were all looking at you? Awful high opinion of yourself, don't you think?"

"Believe me, I don't think I'm a looker," said Finn. I wanted to laugh at how completely wrong he was. He was *gorgeous*. "But on a completely objective level, there was something about me that drew everyone's eyes."

"And what was that?" I asked. His eyes? Was he always as built as he was now, something about his height?

I heard Finn's shower turn off and then his wet footsteps over to the changing area. "I joked about being the Welsh clown of rugby...but you really don't know the nickname they gave me, do you?"

I turned off my shower and picked up the shampoo. I braced myself to step outside. All I had to do was dry myself enough to get my clothes on, and not look up once until Finn was dressed too. Easy.

"Lord of the Lock, right?" I said, carefully avoiding looking over at Finn as I stepped out into the changing area.

"That was my nickname on the field. In the changing rooms and in the bedroom, people started calling me *the Horse*," Finn said casually, like he was reading the weather out.

I reached down for my towel, but without my glasses I managed to knock my forehead on the bench as I did. "Fuck," I

CHAPTER SEVEN - NATHAN

said. I leaned backwards, holding my forehead as stars swam in front of my eyes, and slipped backwards on the tiles, knocking the back of my head on the metal lockers.

"Shit, are you OK?" Finn asked. I was looking down into my own lap and trying to make the black spots in my vision go away.

"Glasses," I said.

"Here." They were thrust into my hand and I did my best to wipe the condensation off them and focus on the floor. Well, my fear at being seen naked had been completely and utterly blown up by the fact I was now laying haphazardly across a cold tile floor with the goods completely on show.

"Nathan, are you OK?" Finn asked. "Look me in the eye, and tell me...I don't know, the current Prime Minister?"

"Who knows," I quipped. "There have been like four this year."

"That's good," he said, "because I don't actually know the answer."

I looked up into Finn's eyes. He was crouched low to the floor, honey-brown eyes staring with concern into mine. And he was stark-bollock naked.

I knew that because my eyes drifted downward as if of their own accord and honed in on...*that.* Finn hadn't been lying when he called himself the Horse. It was hanging below his legs, nestled in a crown of thick, dark pubic hair. He was crouched pretty low on his haunches, and the tip of his cock was almost touching the floor.

"My eyes are up here," he said. I looked up, mortified, but he laughed and held a hand out. "Believe me, it's more of a curse than a blessing."

I took his hand and he pulled me up from the floor. Finn kept one hand on me as he grabbed my towel with the other and laid it out on the bench, then settled me on top of it. He crouched again, but from my higher vantage point it was much easier to focus on just his face.

"Right, how many fingers am I holding up?" he asked.

"Five," I said.

"Good lad," he said. "You should be fine."

"Is that your professional opinion, Dr Roberts?" I asked.

"Don't start playing doctor with me when I've got my willy out, I might get excited," he laughed.

I felt my cheeks heat and realised again how exposed I was. I flipped the towel under me over my groin.

"Insecure?" Finn asked. Finally, he'd caught on to something.

"Yeah, just a bit."

"You shouldn't be. I'm proportional to my height and build. For your height, you're way out of proportion, big boy."

He clapped me on the shoulder and stood up, giving me one last eyeful of the entirety of him. We got changed in silence. When Finn was fully dressed, he walked around to my side of the bench. "Thanks for training with me, Nathan. I'm really enjoying having you around."

8

Chapter Eight - Finn

"Right boys, they don't call me Lord of the Lock for nothing!" I shouted at the motley crew in front of me. "As you all know, in rugby the biggest bastard gets lifted, because he with the longest arms is going to be best placed to scrabble for the ball. So you've got to be strong enough to lift that big bastard! You're in luck though, because Ben is the tallest and he's a fucking string bean of a kid so it's like lifting a feather. Those of you who are normally involved in line-outs, I want you to show me what you've got. Those of you who aren't, I'd like you to line up as an opposition team. As soon as Ben's feet touch the ground, I want you to get that ball by any means."

I watched as the boys lined up for their line-out. They were still hesitant around me but they had raw skill and talent that Rhod had probably nurtured in most of them since they were eight. Ben was like I had been at his age, tall and rangy. He hadn't been involved in many line-outs as a lock, but I had faith in him to be fantastic.

One of the lads held the ball above his hand. "Ready, ready, ready, UP!" I shouted, and Ben was lifted. In a real line-out he'd have to compete with the opposing team for the ball, but the real danger would be when he got to the ground and someone tackled him.

The ball was thrown.

Ben caught it effortlessly.

And then Darren, one of our biggest bastards, rushed him and tackled him before his feet could even touch the ground. Ben went down with the ball and his shoulder just about cushioned the fall before his head connected with the grass.

By the time I got to him Ben was wheezing, the air knocked out of him. I was most worried by the way that his neck had moved as he hit the hard grass. Unusually for this part of Wales, it hadn't rained in a couple of weeks.

"Right everyone, I want you running passing drills." I crooked one finger at the lad who'd tackled Ben. "Darren, come here. For fuck's sake, your tackling is fucking shocking. You never tackle in the air, you could kill someone. Get off my pitch!" A very sad looking Darren jogged away. He was getting no sympathy from me. But the young man lying at my feet was. "You OK, Ben? Your heart still beating?"

"I think so," he said.

"Who's the current prime minister?" I asked.

"How the fuck should I know?"

Fuck. Surely someone could tell me. It had been unanswered on my crossword for days, and I was too ashamed to admit I didn't know the answer. I looked around, hopeful someone smart enough had a concussion. But everyone else was running around practising the defensive tackling drill I'd given them.

"Right, Ben. I'm going to have to ask you not to move. I don't know if you've hurt your neck badly in the fall so I'm going to see if we have someone medically trained around."

"Did someone call for a doctor?" said a familiar, friendly voice.

"You're a physiotherapist," I replied.

"Well I'm the best you've got, so live with it." I turned to face Bernie, Cardiff Old Navy rugby team's physio, who was walking across the rugby field with Garrett Gray, Wales' newest Head Coach.

"What are you two doing here?" I asked, almost dropping Ben's head.

"You asked me to come," said Garrett. "So I came."

"I asked you to visit me like four months ago!"

"I've been busy," said Garrett. Bernie blushed. What the hell was going on there, I wondered.

Bernie knelt down next to me and took Ben's head in his hands. As I stood up to let him do his work, I noticed that the drills had all stopped. "What are you all looking at, get back to work!"

"Well I am pretty handsome," said Garrett, pushing back his famous light blond hair that seemed to get greyer by the day.

"According to whom?" Bernie asked. "Ben, you'll be fine to stand up now. You might have a minor concussion, but I can't see any issues with your neck or head that need immediate fixing. Stay off rugby for the next two weeks though, OK?"

"But the season is less than a month away!" I said. Ben ambled across the field. If I hadn't seen how gangly his legs were before I'd be worried he was seriously concussed, but life for Ben was completely in zig-zags.

"Do I look like I care?" Bernie asked, then looked past me to Garrett. OK, cool. He was making a point with his boss. *Again.* Garrett had put me on the field against Bernie's advice in my playing days and lived to regret it.

"So what are you really both doing here?" I asked.

Garrett sighed. "I wasn't expecting you to go all Sherlock Holmes on my reasoning. I'm just here to watch you coach, OK? I like to see you in action."

Right. So he was playing his cards close to his chest, and the reasoning hurt.

What it seemed like he might be saying is that I was done with playing rugby. And he was looking at me now for what I might want to do next.

"I've been training too, you know," I said, cringing even as the words came out of my mouth. "Y'know, just in case anyone wants to call me back."

"Sure, Finn. I'm not coaching Cardiff any more but I'll put in a good word."

Yep, definitely being frozen out. Nice. "Well, thanks Garrett. I really appreciate it," was my reply.

Even though my heart was sinking, I turned to the lads. "Come on, we've got half an hour left, let's go! It's August, and some of you aren't even sweating!"

"I am!" came one call, and I had to laugh. I had everyone line up and show me their tackling, and I made notes on each. Some of the boys were defensive walls, and I'd be letting Rhod know who I thought should be starting. Plenty of them had gained stamina and speed since I'd set such heavy requirements on them for training.

Once those drills were wrapped up, I sent one of the lads to get the crash pads, and let them go wild with tackling inanimate squishy objects for the last ten minutes. Once they were all done, and sticky with sweat and dust, I sent them to the showers. "Well done all, that's the commitment I want to see in games! One hundred percent!"

CHAPTER EIGHT - FINN

"Yeah, you tell them!" shouted another voice. One I knew well and hadn't realised I'd been missing.

"Hey, stranger," I said. Nathan was stood next to Bernie, his shocking pink hair clashing with the streak of green in Bernie's. Garrett stood about two feet away from the both of them. Nathan's shoulders had rounded out nicely with a few weeks of training and there was definition in his arms that hadn't been there before. If he had been perfect when I first met him, then his physique and confidence in meeting strangers took him to a level no man had seen before.

"Gossips," Garrett muttered as I drew level.

"Been getting on like a house on fire," said Nathan as he held out a pink flask. "Coffee?"

"It's summer!" I said.

"I'm gay, it's iced." Nathan and Bernie high-fived, and I took the flask from Nathan.

"So you didn't tell us you had a boyfriend," Bernie said.

"*Fake* boyfriend," I replied.

Nathan looked scandalised. "So I can't even tell my parents this relationship is fake but you can tell these two random friends?"

"Nathan, Garrett is Wales Rugby Union's head coach, and Bernie is head of physio for Cardiff."

"Oh, um...thank you for your service, I guess."

Garrett laughed. "Do I want to know why you've got an imaginary boyfriend?"

"I'm *right here*," said Nathan. "You can see me. Not imaginary."

"Is fake boyfriend like another way of saying you're friends with benefits? I don't get it," said Bernie. "Or is it like when you're afraid to commit to anything openly because you're scared of what people might think?"

And then he stared right past me with a look that I was surprised didn't kill Garrett on the spot.

"Anyway, we should be going," said Garrett. "Nice to see you Finn, I'll be in touch. Nice to meet you Nathan." He took Bernie by the arm and dragged him away, Bernie giving off a cheery wave as they disappeared behind the stands.

"What was that all about? And why was the coach of a national team here?" asked Nathan.

"I don't fucking know," I replied. "I really don't fucking know."

I took a sip of the coffee Nathan had passed me. "Shit, that's good," I said.

"My friend James buys it in especially for his cafe in Hiraeth," Nathan replied. "Sends it over sometimes in a little care package."

"Do you miss Hiraeth?" I asked.

"I miss my new friends, and I miss *BloodCon*. But I think I'm a city boy at heart. I like being closer to Cardiff. Though I haven't been into Cardiff since I moved back, so maybe I'd be just as well off in Hiraeth again."

"Well. Why don't I see if I can get us some rugby tickets for the Wales friendly in a couple of weeks? Or if not, we could..." I tailed off, well aware I was taking us into actual date territory if I offered to go to for drinks.

"Whatever you like sounds good to me," said Nathan.

"It's a...fate," I said with a stupid cheesy grin and a flourish.

"Fate?"

"Fake date, get it?"

"So you're only asking me out to keep up the illusion, that's what you're saying."

"No, no. I mean..." I had dug myself into a hole. But then Nathan flashed me a grin and nudged my chest. "Just messing with you. I'll look forward." He took step away. "I have to go home and see if Dad's alright, but keep the flask. I'll have it back when I see you next."

When he was another ten or so steps away, a question came to mind. "Why did you come here today?" I asked.

"Well, I had some old fears to get over. And I was thinking of you." Nathan's cheeks blushed the same colour as his hair as he said it, then he turned and walked away, out of sight. I felt a little blush coming on too.

9

Chapter Nine - Nathan

CHAPTER NINE - NATHAN

Trigger warning - Dubious, uncomfortable consent issues, alcoholism. As a flashback, this chapter will be touched upon in later chapters and serves to flesh out Nathan's relationship with rugby and its players, so if you'd prefer to skip it shouldn't hamper your enjoyment of the rest of the book.

8 years ago

Lewis: *Meet me in the woods behind Pandy grounds at 8 2nite?*

That was all he'd sent via Facebook at 3pm. I'd taken hours to decide whether to reply, until I finally had.

Nathan: OK

My heart felt like it was going to explode out of my rib-cage. Lewis was gorgeous, and popular. And he wanted to see me. My little virgin heart couldn't take it. It was a cold, dark and rainy night. Mum and Dad were working in the Pont Hotel, so I had no reason to give them any excuse. They wouldn't be home until well past 11 on a Saturday.

   I pulled my hood up to keep the rain out unsuccessfully, and I was shivering by the time I got to the woods. I turned my phone torch on as I passed through the trees into darkness. I was feeling nervous. Where the hell did he want to meet? How would I find him? Was it going to be just Lewis?

   Then there was a crunch of twigs and a hand on my arm. I spun with the torch in my hand, illuminating Lewis' face, water dripping through his hair and onto him like the last time we had seen one another. He was wearing white shirt, black trousers and the Pandy Rugby Club tie. He'd obviously come right from the rugby club.

"Hey," he said. "Turn off that fucking light. Do you want someone to know we're out here?"

"Sorry," I muttered, turning the phone off so we were stood in darkness. The only illumination was the faint light coming from Pandy rugby club filtering through the trees.

My eyes adjusted as we stood in silence. I was too scared to talk and ruin the moment. I had no idea what Lewis wanted, or why he'd called me out here. I hoped he would kiss me again.

Seconds later, exactly that happened. Lewis' lips met mine in a cold and wet rush, and his tongue pushed into my mouth.. His hands found my face as he pushed me roughly up against a tree. I did my best to keep up with him, but his mouth mashed roughly with mine and his tongue felt invasive. This was *not* what I had imagined kissing a boy would be like. Even worse was the smell and taste of beer invading my mouth.

Even with all that, I was hard, and I could feel him hard and grinding up against me as we kissed. I pushed him off me to get some air.

"C'mon, man. I came to get off." Lewis kissed me again, his hands tangled in my hair. It felt gross, I was shivering. But wasn't this exactly what I'd always wanted.

One of his hands moved from my face, down my neck and along my arm, then guided my hand to his hard on. "C'mon, man. Help me get off. I just want to cum."

10

Chapter Ten - Nathan

Mum was working longer and longer days, and constant care for my dad was starting to piss me off. What was pissing me off even more was my father's insistence that I be with him 24 hours when everything around him had been adapted for him. I'd never anticipated having to bathe my Dad when he wasn't long past fifty years old, but I'd done so multiple times despite the shower-seat that was set up so he could just slide on from his wheelchair, and the bar installed so he could even stand up if he wanted to.

I'd dressed him, prepped his food, and made him a cup of tea. And Mum had closed the Pont for the day as it was so hot outside the chefs were overheating in the kitchen, so he would be alone for less than an hour whilst she wound up. That didn't seem to satisfy him.

"Bloody hell, Nathan. You find a new man and you're suddenly neglecting me. It's not fair and you know it."

I held my tongue, but I imagined my response spearing into him from my mind. *What isn't fair is bringing me back to this shithole and making me wait on you hand and fucking foot, Dad.*

"Dad, I've left you with everything you need. I just need to get out of the house, OK?"

"Then let's go to the Eagle." He smiled.

"I'm going to Cardiff with Finn, I already told you. And you know...you know I don't like the Eagle."

"You left that Lewis boy high and dry, I'm not surprised his friends are out to get you."

"Dad..." I started. I was angry at him. But under all that was a current of sadness. Before he lost his leg, he'd been one of the kindest and most hard-working souls in the world. It was strange to see how the loss had twisted him, made him cruel. "You know things with Lewis weren't right in the end. You know he wasn't nice to me. So I will not be going to the Eagle as long as we know his friends are going."

"Fine, I'll go to the Eagle myself," he said.

"OK, that's fine. Make sure you text Mum to let her know where you're going. I'm glad you're trying to be more independent like the doctors recommended."

His expression soured even more like he thought a threat to go out on his own — which literally everyone had been telling him to do — would make me want to stay home with him.

As I reached the door, I heard him speak again. "If I get knocked down into the road off this wheelchair, Nathan, it's all your fault."

I rolled my eyes, and with just the slightest twinge of guilt, shut the door behind me. He would be fine. He *would* be fine.

When I got to the bus stop Finn was already waiting for me, and the bus was just cresting over the hill. "Everything OK?" he asked as I got near him. I just wanted him to hug me, but I resisted asking. I didn't want to be too needy. We were fake boyfriends, and I didn't need to mix those feelings up when I was still so messed up inside.

"I'm fine. Got the tickets?"

"Tickets? I got us the VIP treatment," Finn grinned as he got onto the bus and paid for both of us. "Where we're going, we don't need tickets."

"O...kay," I said. Finn squeezed his huge body into a bus seat, and I sat down next to him. His legs were angled diagonally because the seat in front was so close to him, and it meant that our legs were pressed up against one another. I was getting over my discomfort around him, and it scared me that I didn't know what that discomfort was being replaced by.

The bus ride into Cardiff got busier and busier, and by the time we finally reached the Central Station people were packed in like sardines and I was pressed even more into Finn's warm side.

The bus emptied and I grabbed Finn's hand automatically to guide him through the huddled mass. As soon as we were off the bus I dropped it. Town was busy and it was hot, the sun beating down on us as we made our way through the crowds. The best thing about being with someone of Finn' size was that the crowd parted around us as he walked through. He was an intimidating figure and people steered clear.

I'd thought I was a city boy at heart but after a year in Hiraeth and months back home in Pontycae, the city felt claustrophobic, and Finn's presence calmed me and kept people away from us.

"So what's the big VIP experience?" I finally asked as Finn led me towards the big, imposing Millennium Stadium.

"You'll see."

I'd never been much interested in rugby, but I'd gone to a couple of matches once upon a time to watch Lewis play in local matches. Finn was vibrating more the closer we got to the stadium like some kind of homing beacon. His excitement was infectious.

We neared a stall selling hats, scarves, flags and Welsh dragon face paint. "Two scarves, please," I said, holding on to Finn's arm to stop myself from losing him in the crowd. The vendor handed over two CYMRU/WALES scarves decorated in dragons and daffodils. I passed one to Finn.

"Nice!" Finn said. "I haven't had one of these since…well, since I started playing for Wales. Didn't need a scarf to watch when I was playing. Thank you."

"No problem." I left the scarf loose over my shoulder because of the warmth of the sun. Perhaps I'd have been better off buying a bucket hat like I'd seen so many others wearing.

"Who's playing today?" I asked.

Finn rolled his eyes. "It's a summer friendly against Georgia. In theory we should smash them, but the squad…" he looked around like a Welsh player was about to jump out of the crowd and accost him. "The squad isn't great. Garrett is new to the job and he's trying for a total refresh, but some of the squad is just that bit too old. We've got great legacy players, but we need more of Rhys. More new blood, more stars."

"They need you," I said.

Finn blushed and looked down at me. "The last thing they need is a PR disaster with dick-sucking tendencies."

It was weird to see him insecure, but it was a side I was getting to see more of. "They'd be lucky to have you back," I said. "You're one of the best players we've ever had."

"What position did I play?" Finn asked me, a grin playing at the edge of his lips.

Shit. I knew he'd mentioned it, but I'd completely forgotten. "Flanker?"

CHAPTER TEN - NATHAN

"You've never seen me play, have you?" he asked.

"Never," I confessed. "I've heard you're very good though. Dad said so after he'd finished moaning about his porridge being too cold."

Finn laughed. "Well I'm glad he's a fan."

Before we reached the big gates and turnstiles that people were pouring through and into the stadium, Finn grabbed my hand and pulled me away. The other hand was on his phone, tapping away rapidly. We walked up to a high cast-iron gate with a ramp that led to a lower level.

"Just have to wait here," he said.

The crowds passed us by, chattering excitedly about the match. A few recognised Finn and did a double take, and I found myself nominated to take pictures of him with fans. Finn made sure to smile for the camera every time, arms around people easy like they were his own family. So many people complimented him on his games, his playing, even asking when he'd be back to play for Wales again. I was watching his confidence grow by the minute.

We'd been waiting for about five minutes when a group of lads walked past, and one of them muttered loud enough to hear, "there's the faggot who got exposed sucking cock on the internet..." before passing us by.

I looked up at Finn. His face had dropped and I hated that someone had taken that smile from his face. I found myself doing something I could never have imagined doing.

"Oi!" I shouted at the group of lads. They all turned in unison. Fear and anger were fighting in me. Even though they were all bigger and stronger than I, it was the anger that won. "Who the fuck do you think you are, talking about someone like that?" I had no idea which of the lads had said it, but I focused my anger on the one in the middle.

"Nath..." Finn said behind me as they approached me.

"You better learn to have some fucking respect. I don't see you and your little beer-belly crew playing for Wales, and I doubt you'd be any good at sucking cock either which means this man already has two achievements under his belt that wankers like you could never hope to match."

I didn't know if it was the crowds, Finn at my back or the police all over Westgate Street, but the four men just tipped their heads with muttered apologies and walked away.

I turned to Finn, determined to do anything to bring that smile back to his face. But he was already grinning. "That was *brilliant*," he said. "It would have been less brilliant if you'd been stabbed, but still. Brilliant."

I sagged against him, all energy and anger gone. I had never stood up to people like that. It wasn't in my nature, and life had always taught me that running was the best possible option.

"Well you looked very impressive doing it," Finn said, squeezing my bicep. "I'm sure you're already looking more muscular."

I knew I was blushing. Luckily I was saved by the creak of the big gate swinging open. "Hey," said Bernie from the other side. "You two ready for the VIP experience?"

11

Chapter Eleven - Finn

The game was going...not great for Wales. But that didn't matter. Because for the first time in a long time, I was struggling to focus on a game of rugby. Rugby was my religion and the Stadium was my church. But I was way too fucking focused on the beautiful man beside me.

"So they have to pass backwards and if they pass forwards, play gets stopped?" Nathan asked.

I nodded. "How do you not know that? That's like the most basic law of rugby."

Nathan grimaced. "I have tried to erase rugby out of my mind. This is fun though." He was watching the game with his glasses halfway down his nose, to *see better*, he'd said.

As Wales slowly advanced toward the try line and a Georgian player ripped the ball from one of our player's arms, Nathan stood up in outrage. "But you said they couldn't do that!"

"I said they couldn't take the ball from someone on the ground that they'd tackled. If the player is being held up in the air, then the opposing team can rip the ball out of their hands."

As we watched that same Georgian player ran the length of the pitch and scored a try. The Welsh home crowd groaned, but nowhere was the disappointment more apparent than behind us. I glanced back at Garrett, who was sat with a face like thunder and talking into his earpiece. "Tell them to get their fucking act together, I could play better rugby than that and I've been retired for years."

"Want me to lace up my boots?" I half joked. Garrett just glared at me like I'd squatted down and shit on his shoe.

"Is Rhys playing? I don't see him," said Nathan.

"No, and I've already mentioned that to Garrett," I muttered. Bernie was pacing behind Garrett and muttering to himself too. I had no idea what he was doing there or why he'd been so attached to Garrett recently. Bernie was Cardiff's head physiotherapist and had nothing to do with the Wales squad.

"What would *you* fucking do then?" Garrett asked me. I hadn't realised he was listening in.

I hesitated before answering. He had been my head coach up until very recently, and he certainly hadn't wanted my bloody opinion then. "...I'd be more defensive, more cautious. It might be really fucking boring to play, to keep passing down the line and hitting a brick wall. But Andy keeps trying to showboat his way past the Georgians and fucking it up for everyone else. Bring Rhys on for the attack, and bring George Reynolds on to be that defensive wall."

Garrett studied me for a second, and I worried I was about to get the biggest bollocking of my life. But then he pressed a finger to his ear and made exactly the call I'd just suggested. Rhys was one of my best friends, but I knew he was good, and I had no idea why Garrett hadn't started him. And George was a recent addition to the team who'd been playing away in France

CHAPTER ELEVEN - FINN

before Cardiff had given him an offer he couldn't refuse. I watched as he ran on, a slower and bulkier player than most modern rugby players. But I knew he could tank a few hits.

And he did. The team played fucking beautifully with my suggestions in place. Even then, I was having trouble keeping a real eye on the game. Nathan seemed extra excited by the fact my play was working, and every now and then he'd grab my arm as Rhys broke through the ranks to score a try, or George kept hold of the ball after another hard hit from one of the Georgian players. Every twinkle in his eye, every cheer, every time Nathan raised that scarf over his head and shouted "Wales!" sent a shock through me. I was so happy to see Nathan enjoying the game.

I watched as Rhys broke through their ranks in the very last seconds of the game and scored a fantastic try, touching down right between the goalposts to make things easier for our kicker. We'd won anyway, and the crowd went wild. Nathan grabbed my arm excitedly and cheered, then leaned in. "We won!! He shouted. "You made it happen!"

And then he pulled me even closer and kissed me. It was quick, in the moment, just a mashing of our lips together in sheer excitement. But in that second the whole crowd faded away.

And then Garrett was punching me on the shoulder to pull me in for a hug and the moment was over. "Fake relationship, huh?" he whispered in my ear.

"Shut up," I muttered back. Because there was just *something* about Nathan that drove me crazy. I turned back to Nathan, who blushed and grimaced up at me.

"Sorry," he said quietly, so quiet I could barely hear him over the crowd.

"Sorry?" I asked. "Why are you sorry?"

"Y'know, the kiss, and..." he tailed off.

"Fake boyfriends, right?" I asked. "Gotta kiss sometimes. Keep up the illusion."

"Yeah?" he asked. I gently took his face in my hands and leaned in toward him, giving him plenty of time to back out or move if he wanted to. But Nathan leaned forward into the kiss and our lips met, so gently and so fucking beautifully that I'd have written poetry about it if I was any good at spelling...or rhyming...or had ever read any poetry.

When Nathan did pull away, the blush was still there but he was smiling. "Good fake."

"Yeah, good fake."

His hand slipped into mine as the crowd slowly dispersed from the stadium. "Could you both stay for a minute?" asked Garrett.

"Sure," I said. "You wanting to congratulate me for winning you a game without even setting foot on the pitch?"

"Something like that," Garrett said. "I'm watching your coaching skills closely, Finn. Just know that."

"Sounds fucking ominous. *I am watching you closely, young Padawan. Strong in the Force you are,*" I said, completely failing at my Yoda impression. Nathan laughed, but Garrett was still stony-faced.

"I'm serious," he said. "Just keep doing well with Pandy and we'll see if you can make the same jump in coaching as you did playing. OK?"

"OK," I said, trying not to show any disappointment on my face for what was a very good deal. "Thank you."

We said our goodbyes to Garrett and Bernie — who was still hovering around Garrett like they were connected with a fucking

CHAPTER ELEVEN - FINN

umbilical cord — and made our way out of the stadium and on to the streets. "Fancy a drink somewhere?" I asked. "Cardiff is busy on game day, but we can see if my face can get us anywhere..."

Nathan hesitated. "Would it be OK if we didn't? Dad's been a nightmare recently, and I worry if I get home too late he will have badgered my poor mother half to death."

"Alright," I said. "No worries."

The bus stops were full of people trying to get home after the match but we managed to barely squeeze on to one bus heading back to Pontycae. Space was so tight that we were pushed up against each other and the Nathan leaned back against me, his face pale. I squeezed one shoulder in a way that I hoped was reassuring and he looked back at me with a tight smile.

"Not good in small spaces?" I whispered.

"Nah," he said back. "Not for me."

We stood for most of the way to Pontycae, finally getting seats as the bus passed through Caerphilly and the majority of the valley-bound passengers got off.

"Are you feeling alright?" I asked Nathan.

He turned to me with a real, genuine smile. "I've had a fantastic time. Honest. I better get home. But thank you for today, Finn. I really enjoyed."

And then he was walking back down the hill towards his house, and out of sight. I hated seeing him go. And I wondered whether, in some crazy world, we would have a relationship that wasn't just an act for everyone else.

12

Chapter Twelve - Nathan

I *had* had a fantastic time. But something in my stomach curdled with the knowledge that there was a deeper liking for Finn than I'd ever like to admit out loud. It had been inevitable, maybe. He was inevitable, and impossible to deny. Not in the same way other men had made themselves impossible to deny, with a quick shove downwards or a grip as hard as iron, but with his sparkling personality, his joy.

It was impossible not to be attracted to Finn Roberts, and it amazed me that the whole world didn't think the same. If I was Wales coach and he'd batted his eyelashes at me and asked for his spot back, I'd be handing him his kit back and telling him to lace on his boots before he could finish asking the question.

Which is why heading home alone from the bus-stop was the best idea at that time. Finn had offered for me to head to his afterwards for a quiet beer but I'd let him down as gently as I could. I needed to be by myself.

As soon as I got home I knew I wasn't going to be so lucky. There were raised voices coming from the kitchen, my mother and father sounded like they were really going at it. Which,

CHAPTER TWELVE - NATHAN

considering my mother had been walking on eggshells since Dad had lost his leg, was a minor miracle.

"Nathan does so much for us, and you just had to go and throw it in his face!" Mum shouted. "You are not the man I married!"

"No, I'm a one-legged old man who needs proper care and attention. If our son isn't going to give me that proper care and attention then he can stop living like a king in this house."

"For fuck's sake..." my mother tailed off as she noticed me standing in the doorway.

"What's going on?" I asked.

"I tried to stop him, I really did," said Mum. "But he'd already made up his mind."

"I've decided I want my office space back," said Dad. "So I've taken the liberty of moving everything for you."

"Just...just go and have a look," said my Mum. She had the same weary tone she'd taken on with almost everything to do with my father.

I rolled my eyes and trooped up the stairs. What had the old twat done now?

I opened the door to the office. It was spotless, the bed was made, and all my packages, all my merchandise...gone. My computer and printer in the corner were gone too.

"What the fuck?" I muttered to myself. I turned to the door into the little box room and pushed it open. It only opened halfway, as the mass of packaging materials and boxes on the bed were stopping the door from being properly opened. Over all the packages, on the bed I could see my computer tower and monitor poking through the mess.

I ran down the stairs two at a time in a rage. "What the fuck have you done?" I asked my father. I didn't know that I'd ever spoken to him like that, but I was furious. "I dropped everything to come here and help you."

"Did you? I thought you were off with some bloke," he deadpanned. "Whereas I'm here, wasting away because I can't get the proper care."

"Then *get* the proper care!" I shouted. "God knows you've had your only son wiping your arse when you still have two capable hands. You managed to shift all those boxes and unplug my computer without calling for anyone's help, didn't you?"

"My mobility is none of your concern," he muttered. "I needed the office back."

"So you're going to help Mum with the business again?" I asked. Dad grimaced. "Apparently not, then. You just did it out of spite."

"You can use the spare bedroom to do business, I'm sure it'll all be fine," said Mum, convincing no-one including herself.

"So I'm sleeping in the office now?"

"You are bloody well not, I might want to use it for late night working," said Dad.

"So there's no space for me to sleep, no space for me to work... right." I turned away from the two of them and walked towards the front door.

"Where do you think you're going?" My father asked.

"Don't start caring where I sleep now," I said without looking back. I opened the door and slammed it as dramatically as I could behind me. I'd never had a proper teenage argument with my parents, so to have it a decade late felt right somehow.

It was still light out, the late summer sun was still warm. But I still felt a tremor rack its way through my body. It was horrible to see a man I'd loved and looked up to becoming so spiteful. I was there and willing to help. I'd dropped everything, my whole

CHAPTER TWELVE - NATHAN

new life, when my parents had asked me to come home. And it seemed my payment was even more misery than the last time. Last time, my home had been my safe space from all the crap that Lewis and his mates put me through.

Now? There wasn't a safe space in the whole village for me. I took my mobile phone out of my pocket and dialled an old friend in Hiraeth.

The phone only rang once before James picked up. "Hey!" he said. "How are things?"

"Miserable," I admitted. "My Dad has basically kicked me out, my ex's mates still have a violent vendetta against me, and I think I fancy someone who's a walking red flag."

"Ouch," said James. "Sounds...not fun. Now isn't the right time to invite you to a wedding, is it?"

"No, but send the invite anyway. I'm glad you and Llywelyn are getting on with it."

"Well we've rented a barn..." as James talked me through his wedding plans, I ambled along the pavement and then sat down on a bench to bathe in the last rays of the summer sun. "...but are you safe?" James asked, and I realised I'd completely zoned out.

"Huh?"

"Are you home safe now? You mentioned your dad had kicked you out and a violent vendetta, I don't want you out at night if there are men round every corner with baseball bats."

I laughed, but it wasn't really funny. "Nah. Don't wanna go home just yet."

"And you can't stay with your walking red flag? What's so bad about him?"

"He's funny, kind, gorgeous, has the biggest penis known to human or horse kind...but he's a rugby player. And he's massive."

"And which part of that is the red flag?"

"Uhh...the rugby player bit? And the fact that he could bend me in half like a pretzel?"

"I'm feeling there's trauma here that you're not telling me about."

"Well..." I started. "I've just not had great experiences with men like him. I ran from this place because of a small-town rugby man who seemed half decent and seemed to like me. I don't want to repeat the same mistake again."

"Can you stay there, just for one night?" he asked. "Does it feel safer than home to you?"

Just for a second, I thought about it. Though I already knew in my heart. Finn was a safe space to me. "Yeah, he's safe."

"Then see if you can stay there for the night."

"I think I will...thanks James."

"Anytime. Text me when you're safe and in the arms of a gorgeous hunk."

I put my phone in my pocket. I felt awful asking Finn for a place to stay, but James was right. I needed to go somewhere I felt I could be safe. If home didn't feel like that, then I needed to find somewhere that would. Just for now. Just for sleep.

I remembered the way to Finn's place, up the hill by the old school to the white house at the end of a row. There was a big garden to the side of his house, and it was getting overgrown. Perhaps he didn't care about the garden.

I knocked on the door. The sun was setting outside and inside there were no lights on, but I heard the shuffle of Finn's feet before he opened the door. He was holding a beer, and I mentally cringed. There was still something about drinking that I couldn't quite shake. But it wasn't Finn's fault.

CHAPTER TWELVE - NATHAN

"Hi, Finn, I, uh..." I got out before the first tear fell. Then another, and then I couldn't stop. Instead of talking, Finn put a gentle hand on my shoulder and gestured me into his house. The door clicked shut behind me, and he flicked lights on as he walked.

"Sorry, I didn't even notice it had gotten dark," he said, leading me into a room that looked like it hadn't been updated since the 70s. The old chintz sofa looked like it would be a squeeze for the both of us, and the wallpaper behind it was a completely different floral pattern that clashed with the whole thing. "Do you want a coffee? Beer? Something stronger?"

"C-coffee would be nice," I managed. I perched on the arm of the sofa, which was ridiculously comfy but had that old-people charity shop smell to it.

"Alexa, make me a Cappuccino please!" he shouted. In the kitchen I heard the sound of coffee being ground.

I laughed through the tears. "You say 'please' to your Alexa?"

"Always polite with women...unless they'd rather I not be," he replied with a devilish grin and a wink that got me laughing even more.

"So what's up? What's got you feeling like this?" Finn asked. When I struggled to get the words out, he headed into the kitchen to grab my coffee and thrust it into my hands before sitting down on the opposite arm, leaving a convenient loveseat-sized gulf between us. He took a swig of his beer. His eyes examined me like they were searching for answers I hadn't given him yet.

So I told him what had happened. I told him my father's attitude and the frustration I'd taken out on him. "Thing is," I said. "Dad was a wonderful, wonderful man before all this. It's not totally his fault that he lost his leg. And I want so badly to believe that the way he's feeling now isn't his fault either. But I'm finding it harder and harder to believe with every passing day. I know how awful this must be for him, but he's always pushed through adversity. But now? It's like he's given up. But he's not just given up, he wants everyone else to give up on him too."

"I feel like you started that whole thing with a psychological question and managed to answer it pretty quickly," Finn chuckled.

"Sometimes, I just need to be allowed to talk," I said. "At home I can't get a word in edgewise."

Finn took another gulp of his beer. "So why here? Just needed a friend to talk to?"

I hesitated. "Well...thing is...I don't want to go home. I was wondering...if I could stay here. Just for one night, to let things cool down."

"Ah. Right." Finn looked around himself for a second. "That's fine, it's just..."

It seemed it was his turn to hesitate, and I wondered if he was looking for an out. "It's fine if you can't, honestly-" I started.

"It's just I only have my bed," Finn cut in. "This sofa's tiny and I don't think I have any spare blankets, and upstairs...well, I never really properly moved in. This was never meant to be somewhere I came back to live."

"That's fine, that's fine," I said. "Honestly. No worries at all. I'll go."

"Stay." Finn said. He didn't move from his spot on the arm of the sofa. "I have a king-size and we can put up a pillow wall between us if you want to to stop me cuddling. Don't have to do any real boyfriend stuff, fake boyfriend."

Those red flags were flapping gently in my head but I had to

CHAPTER TWELVE - NATHAN

remind myself that Finn wasn't anyone else. He was his own person.

"Did you want to go up now, or..." Finn gestured at the sofa. "I was thinking of maybe having a *Thrones of Blood* binge over the next couple of hours."

"So first you tell me you don't want to do anything naughty and now you're telling me you want to Netflix and Chill?" I asked. I hadn't really turned his innuendos back on him before, and it was great to watch a bit of blush creep into his cheeks as he mentally reeled himself back.

"Well, actually chill in this case," Finn said, holding up one hand. "Scout's promise."

"*Then Thrones of Blood* sounds very good to me."

"Shall we actually get comfortable?" Finn asked. "No pressure, I can grab a dining chair to sit down in or something like that, it's just weird us both perching on the arms of the sofa like parrots." He slid down from the arm onto the sofa and patted the space next to me. An invitation with no pressure.

The sofa was tiny, more of a loveseat, so when I slid down from the arm and onto the seat we were touching as closely as we had on the bus. Finn's left arm was wedged against my side, and though he tried to move his legs away it was pointless.

"It's fine, you know. I'm not made of glass."

"I know, it's just...I've noticed you don't like to be touched," said Finn.

"Not all the time. But sometimes. It's...complicated. But you are...you're a safe space, Finn. I'm starting to feel safer around you than by myself."

Finn's grin almost split his face in two it was so wide. "Thanks, Nathan. I really appreciate that."

He grabbed the remote and put the first episode of *Thrones of*

Blood on the TV. I'd watched it so many times now it was unreal.

The whole show opened with Daniel's character kneeling shirtless on the beach, and his wrists chained behind him. "The things I'd do to that man..." Finn muttered.

I laughed. "His boyfriend would tear your head off. Somehow, he's just as gorgeous too. In a pokey small town way."

"Damn it. They looking for a third? Or even just an audience?"

"I should've known you were after a threesome," I joked.

Finn's arm snaked over my shoulders slowly, and I realised I actually liked it. "I've been there, done that enough times," Finn said. "I'm more a one man or woman kinda guy now. That and I can't have people thinking I'm cheating on my *totally real boyfriend*."

I settled into his embrace. "Better not cheat on me, I'm worth more than that."

"You really, really are," said Finn. I felt my cheeks heat up and we sat mostly in silence and together for three episodes of *Thrones of Blood*. Every time a scene filmed in Hiraeth came up or I had any gossip from Daniel about the cast and crew, I brought it up to Finn and he'd smile. After three episodes his yawns were getting louder and more frequent.

"Ready for bed?" he asked.

I nodded, not as easily now. I followed Finn up the dark stairwell to his room. Thankfully, his bed was massive, probably the only new piece of furniture in the house. Finn stripped to his boxer-briefs and hopped in. For a second, I struggled to take my eyes off his broad, furry thighs. But I dragged my eyes up to meet his. "I always sleep on the left," he said when I hesitated. When I didn't step forward, he frowned. 'Is there anything wrong?"

"No, no. Nothing wrong." I pulled my t-shirt over my

head and let my jeans drop, and he looked away respectfully even though he'd probably seen so much more when we were changing. Finn was a good guy. My complex was my problem to deal with.

I climbed into the bed and laid on the opposite side to Finn, almost at the very edge. He radiated heat like a furnace through the blanket. "Alexa, light off, pretty please!" he shouted. We were plunged into darkness. "Night, Nathan," he yawned.

"Goodnight, Finn." I dropped off to sleep in seconds.

13

Chapter Thirteen - Nathan

CHAPTER THIRTEEN - NATHAN

Trigger warning - Dubious, uncomfortable consent issues, alcoholism. As a flashback, this chapter will be touched upon in later chapters and serves to flesh out Nathan's relationship with rugby and its players, so if you'd prefer to skip it shouldn't hamper your enjoyment of the rest of the book.

8 years ago

Prom had been weird. I'd spent the whole night sneaking glances at Lewis with his prom date, and he had kept catching my eye and looking away like we were in the world's most subtle game of cat and mouse.

I had finally caught up with him when he snuck out the back of the hotel we'd had our sixth form prom in to have a secret swig of vodka by himself from a plastic hip flask.

"You OK?" I asked him.

Lewis fumbled and almost dropped the vodka. "Fuck, man you scared me. Want some?"

I took the vodka that he'd been swigging like water and took a sip. I spluttered as the horrible burning sensation touched my throat. "Fucking hell, how are you drinking that?" I asked as I handed the bottle back.

"Dunno, used to it I guess," he said. He took another swig and stepped close enough that I could smell it on his breath. He looked furtively around like he was scared of something and then he kissed me quickly, tongue slipping into my mouth and teeth clattering together. He pulled back and looked around again in case anyone else had come outside.

"We still on for tonight?" he asked.

"Yeah, of course."

"Good. See you later." He threw the hip flask into the bushes and went back inside.

* * *

I had been waiting so long for this, but for some reason my stomach curdled with a sense of dread. I kept looking out of my bedroom window and finally saw Lewis making his way down the street. I took another sip of wine. I wasn't as big a drinker as he was, but I enjoyed the odd glass of wine. It made me feel like a very grown-up eighteen year old to have a few civilised glasses with Mum and Dad in the weekday, rather than heading out to get pissed at the rugby club like Lewis and his mates. Not that I thought I'd be welcome there anyway.

But my parents were out for the weekend, and as I made my way down to the door to let Lewis in my stomach twisted with the thought of what might happen tonight. Lewis and I had a few fumbles in the woods or even in the old rugby stands at night when it had been raining heavily. This would be the first time we had a bedroom to ourselves for the night. I knew that might mean that more would happen between us than usual.

I opened the door and Lewis hurried in. He was still dressed in his prom suit and his tie was loose around his neck. "Close the fucking door then, it's freezing," he said. I closed the door and immediately his lips were on mine. His lips tasted like vodka and sweat, and there was a lipstick stain at the edge of his mouth.

"Were you kissing Gwen?" I asked between kisses.

"What does it matter?" came the muffled reply before he was kissing me again. "Where's the bedroom?"

I took his hand and led him upstairs. His grip was clammy, and when I looked back at him he was still looking around like someone might jump out from the shadows.

"It's just us," I told him. "We've got the house to ourselves

CHAPTER THIRTEEN - NATHAN

for the night."

"Good," he muttered. I led him into my bedroom, lit as it was by Death Star shaped lamp in the corner.

"Well this is fucking nerdy, innit?" Lewis poked at the Death Star lamp. "Queer and into stuff like this, no wonder you don't have many friends."

"Thanks, I guess," I replied.

"Nah, no offence like. Just saying it like I see it." Lewis's lips were back on mine before I could respond and his hands were fumbling with his belt, then fly before his trousers and boxers dropped to the floor. I pulled my own trousers down and I could feel his half-hard length pushing up against my boxers, so I took him in hand as he kissed me more. His hand brushed over my bulge but didn't make any move to do much more with it. I knew my place in our trysts. I did the touching, the pleasuring. I could finish myself off later.

But that's why I was so excited for tonight. If he was going to fuck me, I'd finally get that feeling in return.

Lewis was unbuttoning his shirt, and I did mine too. He pulled it off, leaving him stood in just the tie. I was in my boxers, and I quickly shrugged them off. Lewis glanced down at me briefly before we were kissing again and I was being pushed back onto the bed.

Lewis' arms caged me as he pushed my legs upward onto his shoulders, and for the first time since we'd met I wondered how naive and inexperienced this uber-confident rugby player actually was. He was rutting up against me

"So I just push in, right?" he asked, notching himself up with me.

"Fucking hell, Lewis!" I scrambled backward as he pushed and he collapsed on to me, pinning me to the bed.

89

"What? What did I do wrong?"

"You think you can just go in with no preparation?"

"Oh yeah," he said. He spat in his hand and put his hand over his cock. "Just like they do in porn."

"No, not like they do in porn!" I rolled over to grab the lube from my bedside table. "Use this."

"Oh. Do I have to...touch you, or..."

"Let me sort myself, you sort yourself," I huffed. I had practised with a couple of fingers before and knew vaguely the process of relaxing myself. I took the lube from him and used it to slick up two fingers. Lewis looked vaguely nauseous as I did. Once I nodded at him, he pushed my legs back up and looked down to line himself up.

"Right, let's try this, " said Lewis,

* * *

I had a restless sleep with Lewis' head on my chest, and my stomach was churning. I knew that losing my virginity wasn't necessarily going to be a great thing, but...there was something about being caged in by Lewis' arms as he'd clumsily jackhammered for twenty minutes until he'd said *"I'm too buzzed, mate. Not gonna finish"* that made the whole experience feel a bit shit. And then the fact he'd rolled over and started snoring without asking me if I'd like any help made me feel any worse. Not that I'd still been hard at that point.

And now I felt claustrophobic as his naked form sweated up against me, our clothes still strewn across the floor. I almost wished we never had bothered with tonight. But...there were no take backs now. That was it. It was done. Never getting that back. And I knew that come the morning we could both forget it had ever happened and I would make myself strong enough to resist him. I'd be moving away for university in just a few short months.

"What on earth?" my mother's voice rocked the room, startling me awake. Lewis had crept even further over me in the night, and I instinctively screeched and threw him off as my mother stood in the doorway in the early morning light. Lewis tumbled to the floor, completely naked, as I clutched the covers up and over myself.

"Wha-wha's app'nin," Lewis slurred. And then his eyes snapped open and he seemed to remember where he was. He covered his dick with one hand as he hopped around the room, swearing and trying to find his boxers.

"I *said*, what the hell is going on?" Mum repeated. And Lewis stopped. Just stood there, with his hands covering very little sea looking at her like his life was over.

"This is Lewis," I said. I steeled myself for what I was about to say next, knowing it would fuck us both up. "My boyfriend."

Lewis looked even more horrified than he already had.

14

Chapter Fourteen - Finn

There was nothing better, I thought, still half asleep and content, than waking up warm with my body wrapped around another man. That bedroom smell on skin in the early morning, the soft snuffles of early morning snoring...

"Get off, get off, get off!" I was woken properly by a shout, and suddenly I was tumbling out of bed. My elbow connected with the floor first and I howled as I rolled across thinly carpeted floor. As I rubbed my arm and tried to open my eyes properly, a shock of pink hair came into my vision. "Sorry, so sorry!" Nathan's grey eyes were wide with concern. "...just, nightmare, sorry."

I looked up at him in a daze, my brain still not working. "Nightmare? What were you, sumo wrestling?"

"...something like that," replied Nathan. The smile I'd seen a few times the night before wasn't there in the morning, and I wanted that to change.

"Want to talk about it?" I asked. "Something on your mind?"

"No, no. It's fine."

It was not fine, and I could tell just looking at him. "Scoot

CHAPTER FOURTEEN - FINN

over," I said. "Back to your side of the bed."

Nathan's head disappeared from view as he shuffled over to his side, and I pushed myself up with my good arm to lay next to him, not quite touching. His body was beautiful, pale in the morning sunlight with just the hint of muscle tone to it now. His banana-print boxers were also adorable. But now wasn't the time to be focusing on that.

"Lay on your side," I said, "face away from me."

Nathan looked confused but turned so that he was facing away. I kept my eyes trained on the back of his head, determined not to look any lower.

"Do I have your permission to touch you?" I asked.

"Like how?" Nathan asked, his voice tinged with concern.

"Just one finger on your back," I said. "I won't go anywhere you don't want me to."

Nathan sighed. "Go ahead."

I touched one finger to the back of his neck and drew a gentle line down his spine. Nathan shuddered. "Want to tell me about your nightmare?"

I traced circles around each spot on his spine, stopping a respectful distance from the line of his boxers before working my way back up. After a minute, Nathan sighed and started to talk. "That ex I told you about…we were kids, really. I know we were eighteen, but they don't teach you gay sex ed at school. So I'd done all the research online and he only had experience watching porn. So he wasn't the most…considerate lover."

I bristled, but kept my tone calm. "Did he ever hurt you?"

"No…not deliberately," said Nathan. "I consented to everything, it was all…I don't know, it was legal. I guess that's how I'd put it. But after my parents found out and I told them he was my boyfriend, it was like we settled into this routine. He would come over a few times a week after a few drinks with the lads, and we'd have sex. He would finish sometimes, often not...and then he'd fall asleep, beer on his breath and usually on top of me. I could sort myself out in the bathroom, but I think that aspect of being gay kinda grossed him out."

I willed my finger not to hesitate as I carried on creating relaxing patterns on his back. Nathan was opening up, and much as it was horrible to hear, he needed to say it. "So we carried on for a bit like that...and I didn't know how to get out. Every time I fell asleep, I felt that little bit more claustrophobic or trapped, and I haven't really liked it since."

"So you're not a cuddler?" I asked.

"I...wait." Nathan turned over to face me. "Can you turn over like I did for you?"

I did without asking him why. After a second, he spoke, even quieter and more hesitant than before. "Can I...can I move closer?"

"Of course," I breathed.

After a second, Nathan's hands snaked around my chest, and his body connected with mine. In order for us to spoon, his head was tucked somewhere between my shoulder blades and his feet were still about half a foot further up the bed than mine, but we fit together in that way like an odd jigsaw. I did my best not to be hyper-aware of the way his crotch was pressing up against my arse.

"I've always wanted to do this," Nathan said.

"What, cuddle?"

"No, well, yeah. Big spoon."

"You're still a little spoon, " I teased as his hands idly stroked my chest and stomach, pushing through dark curly hairs and making goosebumps appear wherever they went. "Just like a

CHAPTER FOURTEEN - FINN

teaspoon in the tablespoon drawer, bumping up against the back of a big spoon."

"Whatever, it's nice," replied Nathan, his voice muffled just a little bit by the way his face was smushed between my shoulder blades.

"So we're fake boyfriends with real cuddles?" I asked him after a minute.

"I guess so," said Nathan. He trailed one hand across my stomach and belly-button, and this time I couldn't stop myself from a full on shudder. "Sorry, is this OK?" he asked.

"More than OK. Your hand just feels really good," I said. I was aware that I was getting hard, but didn't want to pull attention to it. Nathan was just starting to trust me, just starting to feel safe around me. That was much more important than getting off. The feel of his hand on my front and warm body at my back were just so, so good. "You know if you need...this kind of thing, no judgement, no fear, I'm here. Cuddle buddy for life."

"No one's ever gotten me talking before like you did just then, " said Nathan after a second. "After all the...shame of everything, I just kept quiet. But you opened me right up."

"I stole it from my therapist," I admitted.

"You got into bed with your therapist?" Nathan asked.

"No, when I struggled to open up she told me to turn away, face the wall. When I couldn't focus and still wouldn't talk she got me one of those fidget toys. It helped take away the tension of talking to a stranger about my problems, just being more focused on that. So I figured if I could take your attention away from the bad thoughts you'd be able to talk more openly about it all."

"You're a very smart man, Finn Roberts."

"Am not. You should see my spelling," I said.

"Smart isn't about what they said to you at school, you know?" Nathan said. "It's about emotional intelligence. Figuring out things for yourself. Pushing through adversity even when you're hurt."

"Well, I got into therapy after the whole video thing wrecked me," I admitted. "I was pretty damn emotionally stupid before then."

"Face me?" muttered Nathan, moving away from me a little bit to give me the room to turn over. I felt my cheeks get warm, knowing what effect his hand had on me. Not wanting to show him.

I tried my best to think of *anything* that would turn me off. Kittens dying. Granny porn. That one scene in *Thrones of Blood* where Daniel Ellison had had to scoop his own guts back into his stomach. But no. Nothing. The knowledge that Nathan was lying almost naked in my bed was enough to keep me at full mast.

"Aren't you going to face me?" Nathan asked.

I had to tell him. With all he'd just told me, I wasn't going to turn without talking first. I didn't want him to see my state as some kind of gross reaction to his emotional trauma. "The cuddles got to me a bit there." I admitted. "If I turn over, I need you to know that I'm not...I'm not coming on to you or anything. It's just a natural reaction to the cuddles."

Nathan laughed quietly. "Are you that worried...that you're hard?"

"Yes," I muttered.

"Just turn over, I've seen it all before," he said.

So I did, slowly and reluctantly and trying to ignore the fact that turning over to face Nathan would make me even harder. That feeling his eyes on me might make the weight in my boxer-

CHAPTER FOURTEEN - FINN

briefs even more obvious.

I looked into Nathan's deep grey eyes in the morning light. And just for a second, they flicked downwards.

"Jesus Christ, man. How the fuck can you have a cock as big as you do flaccid and still be a grower?"

I looked down at my own cock like it was a surprise to me too, but I knew how big I was. The guys in the changing room liked to call me the Horse. Most lovers liked to call me a *challenge* or *not going near that fucking thing.* I was a bit of a trophy or a bragging right in certain circles in Cardiff, and I'd liked that once upon a time.

My cock was straining against my boxers as it curved over one thigh, the size of it lifting at the waistband so that just a sliver of it was visible. I knew Nathan had seen. I looked back up at Nathan, then allowed myself the grace to do the same to him. To my surprise, he was making a pretty big tent in his boxers too.

"Busted," he muttered. "This is weird, isn't it?"

"Only if you want it to be," I replied. We were inches way from one another. We could reach out and touch one another, or we could kiss with a tiny movement of our heads. But we didn't.

"So how far does this...fake relationship go?" Nathan asked. "We're putting it out there that we're together, but we're not? So...is all of this stuff off limits?"

"What would you like?" I asked. "Did you want to...change the deal?"

"Like I told you...my only real sexual experiences have been in a high-pressure relationship, where the sex was bad and I didn't always feel safe. You feel like the opposite, Finn. You're a safe place."

I knew I was blushing, but I could see that same pink creeping into Nathan's cheeks before he continued. "So I'm wondering if we can flip the script on what I had before. If we're not in any kind of relationship, and there's no pressure..." Nathan tailed off.

I was waiting to hear what he had to say, even as my eyes memorised every bit of his body. From the tiny patch of chest hair in the very centre of his chest to the abs that had started to become clearer very early on in our workout sessions to the trail of light brown hair that led from his bellybutton into his boxer shorts.

Finally Nathan spoke. "I was wondering if you'd be a safe space for me to try things again. It's been a while...and it looks like you need it as much as I do." He gestured down at my boxers, where my hard on had subsided a little bit through our conversation.

"That..." I didn't know what to say. My trust in sex had been shot to hell since the video of me had come out and pushed me even further down the spiral I was on. But Nathan was right. This felt like a safe space. This room, just the two of us. "...sounds good to me," I barely said before we were both moving in to kiss.

We both probably had morning breath, and messy hair, and smelled like sleep...but I didn't care. I had Nathan's sweet lips on my own, and it felt amazing. I trailed my finger down his chest but stopped short of his boxers before trailing it back again. This was a safe space for him, and I wouldn't be doing anything without asking his consent first.

Nathan pulled away from the kiss and looked at me. My cock was straining against my boxers again, and there was a damp patch starting to show where I was already leaking. It really had

CHAPTER FOURTEEN - FINN

been too fucking long. Nathan laid back so that we were lying side by side, almost clinically. Slowly, carefully, he pulled down his banana-print boxer briefs to reveal what was underneath. Surrounded by carefully trimmed light brown hair, his cock curved up onto his belly, a tiny bead of pre-cum clinging to the end of it as he pulled his foreskin back over the head slowly.

I could see his whole body shaking as he did, and when he spoke his voice was quivering — with excitement or nerves I didn't know. "Just me, then?" he said with a shaky laugh.

"S-sorry, I just..." I didn't finish my sentence. I had never been so fucking entranced by someone else before. I'd fucked. God, I'd fucked so many people so many fucking times. But Nathan's smooth white body was taking my breath away. I was almost glad he was laying next to me, because if we got the chance to kiss, of him to press his naked body up against mine? I had no idea how my body would react.

Feeling more nervous than I ever had in my life, I played with the waistband of my boxer-briefs before pulling them down, revealing my cock. I hadn't had any action in a while and hadn't bothered to do much tidying up. It was surrounded by a thick nest of dark curls that connected with the snail trail that ran up my body and fanned out into a dark mat of chest hair I'd never been able to tame. Next to Nathan's trimmed perfection, despite my size, I felt inadequate.

Without thinking, I swiped along the slit to gather up the salty, sticky pre-cum and brought it to my mouth. Next to me, Nathan's breath hitched for a second. And hearing that reaction was so fucking sexy.

"Is this...OK?" I asked quietly.

"More than OK," Nathan whispered back. I watched as he pulled back the foreskin again and then brought it back over the pink head of his cock, and a clear bead of pre-cum gathered there. I did the same and slowly we both picked up the pace, like we were keeping time with one another. I wanted more, wanted to put my mouth on his cock or to have his on mine but I knew it wasn't my job to push. Whatever Nathan asked for, he'd get. But he had to ask for it.

"You're so big," Nathan breathed as he worked at his cock, precum now glistening over the head.

"I know," I joked back. "It's a big old problem."

I stroked myself with my right hand and let my left fall to my side, and Nathan was stroking himself with his left. Our fingers touched and somehow that felt more intimate than anything else than anything else I'd ever done. It was like our electricity sparked between our fingers as they brushed against one another. I twitched my fingers and felt him do the same, like we were itching to get closer.

"Not gonna last," Nathan whispered.

"Come. Come for me," I said. The slick noises of Nathan's frantic movements were so hot that they risked pushing me over the edge as he finished, spilling over his hand and on to his stomach.

"Fuck," I said, working my hardest to catch up with him.

"Can I....?" Nathan raised his right hand. "Can I touch you?"

"Please," I replied. Nathan stretched out his hand, gliding over my belly. As soon as his fingers got to my cock and wrapped around the base, thumb and forefinger barely meeting around my girth, I was finishing too, cum coating both of our hands and landing in my pubes and on my stomach.

I was breathing heavy, and risked a glance at Nathan. He smiled shyly back, removing his hand from me and bringing it to his lips. He poked his tongue out to lick the cum on his hand.

CHAPTER FOURTEEN - FINN

"Round two?" I asked, and he laughed.

"God, I need a shower," Nathan said. He looked down at himself and over at me. "You do too."

"Would you like to shower with me?" I asked. "No pressure if that feels too much..."

"No, I'd love to," he said. I got up off the bed and gestured for him to follow - we both did the awkward hobble-dance of *please don't let this cum drip on the carpet* on our way to the bathroom, and I turned on the shower as quickly as I could. The bathroom was as old-fashioned as the rest of the house, and the shower had been adapted as a big walk-in for my gran before she passed. That was lucky for us as it meant that even with my stupid-sized body we could still fit in comfortably.

I tested the water before stepping under. Nathan followed me and stood by as I washed most of the cum out of my body hair with just water.

"Stop hogging the water," he said, giving me a gentle shove to get under the spray. Even though I was completely sexually satisfied from wanking with him, the sight of his smooth, pale body under the water made my dick twitch.

Nathan noticed that I was sporting a semi and laughed. "Down, boy."

"Hypocrite," I said, looking at where he was starting to stand to attention again. "Can I...help you wash?"

"As long as that's all you're after," said Nathan, smiling so I knew he really was OK with it. I grabbed the shower gel from the rack and washed Nathan's back, doing my best not to linger for too long on his perfect, firm arse.

"Turn around," I whispered.

"I can do my front," he protested.

"Well so can I if you'll let me," I responded. I took my hands away from him to let him decide if he wanted me to, and then he turned to face me and shrugged. I soaped up his chest, then drew my hands down his arms to his hands before washing his stomach and around his semi-hard cock. I got to my knees, and he let me wash his legs and feet gently. I had seen so many naked bodies in my time, fucked so many men and women, and yet I'd never wanted to be so close to someone before. I wanted to put my heart in his hands and trust him to never fucking let it go.

But Nathan had been hurt, and I was here to give him protection in the outside world and a safe space on the inside. It wasn't my job to push him into a real thing he'd been clear he didn't want.

Nathan put one finger under my chin and tilted my head up to look at him. "You OK in there?" he asked.

"I'm…all good." I realised I'd been on my knees and in my own little world as I thought.

"My turn," said Nathan. That finger stayed as a gentle pressure under my chin as I stood, and Nathan squirted the shower gel onto his hand before reaching upward to massage it into my chest. He tangled his fingers into the covering of hair and stroked down through it all to my belly.

I felt a little bit self-conscious. "I used to shave all that, kept myself smooth….I've let myself go a bit," I admitted.

Nathan's hand ghosted past my cock and brushed against the hair there. "I like it like this," he said. "Turn around."

I did as I was told and felt as Nathan's hands washed down from my shoulders, into the divots at the bottom of my back and finally cupped my arse more suggestively than I had dared to with him. I knew I wasn't exactly smooth back there either but Nathan washed it pretty thoroughly so he must have liked it.

"Back around?" Nathan asked I turned to face him and he captured my face in his hands under the spray before standing on his tiptoes. I closed the distance between us and kissed him with wet lips under the shower spray. "Thank you," he said.

I should have been thanking him. Instead, I just kissed him again.

15

Chapter Fifteen - Nathan

I felt like a teenager, sneaking back in to my parents' house after a night out with a man. The difference being, I felt like I was coming home *clean* now. And not just because Finn had showered and worshipped every inch of my skin. Every time I'd ever had sex with a man — and it had only ever been one particular man — I couldn't help but feel dirty afterwards, my stomach churning with the feeling that we were doing something *wrong* somehow. And now, finally, I was kind of starting to see why.

Lewis and I had been two inexperienced kids when we'd met, and Lewis' self loathing had rolled off him in waves. It had infected me, a little nerd otherwise happy with his sexuality. It had made me hate the one thing I most wanted. And with a safe space like Finn, it had been different.

So I was practically whistling as I stepped into the kitchen, only stopping when I noticed that Mum was already sat down at the breakfast bar with a cup of tea. "You OK, love? You had us worried," she said.

"Who's us? Dad was the one who essentially kicked me out,"

CHAPTER FIFTEEN - NATHAN

I said.

"Well..." Mum waved one hand about in the air hopelessly. "I was worried. And he probably would be too, if he were in his right mind."

"But he's not, Mum. It's not fair on you and it's not fair on me."

"What do you want me to bloody do about it?" Mum snapped. And then her face crumpled into a frown. "Sorry, sorry. I'm just so stressed because..."

"Because Dad is being a prick. I know. I know."

"Where did you stay then? You weren't answering your phone..."

"With Finn," I replied as casually as I could, hoping the blush didn't creep into my cheeks. *Why do I even care? Everyone thinks we're going steady anyway.*

"So things are going well for you then?" Mum asked. "I mean, after the last boyfriend...I thought you'd sworn off his type for life. Your father said who it was, that Welsh rugby player who was in all the papers months ago."

"Finn isn't that type, Mum. He's...nice." It was nice, not having to lie about our relationship for her. All I was saying was true. Finn was a nice guy, and I enjoyed spending time with him.

Why isn't he my boyfriend? The thought crossed my mind. I mentally swatted it away. Neither of us was in the right place mentally to commit to that kind of thing.

"So, your boyfriend. When do I get to meet him?" Mum asked.

"Well I'm not bringing him here," I said. "Not with Dad being the way he is about everything."

"The Pont then, I'll set you both up a table this evening if he's free. It'll be a date, you'll hardly know I'm there, I just want to see...I want to see that you're safe, Nath."

That almost broke my heart. Unlike Dad's new flippant attitude towards Lewis, Mum seemed to still know how much that whole part of my life had shaped and hurt me. And how it had pushed me away. "I'll text him and see if he's free."

"Good. I'm glad..." Mum tailed off as a banging noise on the ceiling up above us made us both wince. "Your father's awake, I should go and see what he wants."

"We need to talk about what to do with him," I said. "In the nicest way possible, he's making our lives shit right now."

Mum snorted. "The nicest way possible, of course. What can we do? He's your father, my husband."

"Not the same one I remember. He needs help, Mum. And not just from us. Professionals. You deserve a break, and he's clearly trying his best to piss me off at the moment."

"He's not doing it on purpose, love," Mum said. "He's just struggling with all this. The change he's gone through, losing a leg and his dignity-" The banging interrupted her again. "God forbid he uses his crutch for *something*," she muttered as she left the kitchen. And I was left none the wiser as to how to help her.

I pulled out my phone to text my not-boyfriend, who was nonetheless saved in my phone with a heart emoji next to his name like I was some stupid lovestruck teenager.

Nathan: Hey fake boyfriend, wanna be my fake date and get real good food tonight?

Finn: I thought you'd never ask.

CHAPTER FIFTEEN - NATHAN

The Pont had come on leaps and bounds since my parents had taken it over. It had once been a social club and bar like so many others in the Valleys, but they were dime-a-dozen and the clientele was shrinking rapidly. They'd worked together on this labour of love to bring it more upmarket, to turn it into something Pontycae was sorely missing. They'd repainted the walls, polished the floors, brought in new artwork and a chef from Cardiff, but the shape of the old bar was still present.

Some of the old clientele still sat on stools next to the old bar in the corner and ordered pints from the minute they finished work until they had to go home to their wives and children. But that crowd was growing old and dying out, and the Pont Hotel was for the most part an up-and coming gastropub with all the fancy new-age quirks that brought. I was sat on a tiny table in one corner of the room, lit by the flicker of a cold electric candle. My mother was stood behind the bar coordinating staff about on this busy night, and every time I looked over she was looking at me. Waiting for the chance to meet my man.

I noticed Finn as soon as he stepped into the room. But then again, pretty much everyone did. He was huge and gorgeous, and dressed to impress in a shirt that hugged close to his body in a way that made me jealous I wasn't a shirt.

I waved at him from my little table, and the way his eyes lit up when he saw me made me think that perhaps he was almost as pleased to see me as I was him. He made his way through the restaurant, all eyes on his massive frame as he edged between tables and just about avoided knocking things over. He was surprisingly graceful for a man with a body that would make Bigfoot feel inadequate.

"Evening," he said as he slipped into his chair.

"How's your day been?" I asked.

"Good, actually. Rhod asked me to take on an extra team activity so my diary is filling up, but it's good to keep busy. Keeps my mind and my hands occupied." Finn picked up the wine list to have a look. "What do you drink? Sorry, I've never really asked."

"I don't," I confessed. We'd been honest with each other so far, and he didn't feel like the kind of person to pressure that information out of me. "In my old relationship, things got complicated by drink. I stopped not long after I moved away permanently."

"Oh, sorry. I can avoid drinking around you if you'd like." Finn put the menu away hastily and almost knocked over the salt and pepper shakers.

"No, no there's no need," I said. "Honestly. It's a me problem, not a you problem."

Finn seemed unsure what to say to that, but he was saved from having to reply by the presence of my mother, holding a notepad and dressed in much smarter managerial wear than I'd ever seen her wearing in the Pont Hotel. "What can I get you both to drink?" she asked.

"Finn, this is my mum Tina, Mum, this is Finn."

"Nice to meet you," Finn stuck his hand out for Mum to shake.

Mum took his hand and shook it. "And what are your intentions for my son?"

"Could you be any more cliché?" I groaned as Finn turned a deep red. We both knew that our intentions were anything but honourable, especially compounded by recent activities. We were living a lie and living in sin. So shoot us.

"Just....seeing where things go," he muttered. He made eye contact with me under heavy brows, and I had to do all I could to keep myself from laughing.

CHAPTER FIFTEEN - NATHAN

"I see," Mum said. "So, drinks?"

"Lime and soda for me please," I said.

"Same for me," said Finn. Mum nodded and headed back behind the bar before I could ask him if that was *really* what he wanted.

"How come you're not drinking?" I asked. "You don't have to stop on my account."

"I'm stopping tonight on *my* account," said Finn. "It's way too easy to get into a bit of a routine with drink, and I think that's what I've been doing recently."

"Fair dos. What are you thinking of, food-wise?" I asked. "I used to help with cooking until Mum noticed that I was stealing more chips than I was serving. Then I got put on waiter service, but I was such a quiet kid that I didn't exactly endear myself to customers."

Finn laughed. "Thank God you went into a business that requires customer service skills round the clock then."

"Why do you think I kept my shop mostly online? I might be quiet in person but I send a fantastic fucking email. Anyway, food?"

Finn perused the menu. "Steak any good here?"

"The best. But I'm a fan of fish, personally. The chef does a mean salmon."

Finn's nose wrinkled. "Sirloin steak for me then, I'm not much of a fish fan."

Another waitress came over with our drinks and took our food orders. Obviously Mum had seen enough of Finn to trust someone else to deal with him now. I was just thankful for the lack of awkwardness.

"How's Pont's chances looking for the season coming up?" I asked. I had no real interest in rugby, but seeing Finn's enthusiasm for it always made me happy.

"The men's team has the derby match with Pandy first thing in the new season," said Finn. He took a sip of the soda before carrying on. "Thing is, I'd normally be really confident in our chances. We finished last year top of the league, we've got a little bit of professionalism within the team whereas they're completely amateur...but the derby match is always going to scare me. They really fucking try hard to beat us. And they've got some big bastards on the team who could make mincemeat out of us if they really wanted to."

"Training much then?" I asked. "Surely you're working around everyone who has jobs..."

"I've got the men's and women's team training twice a week each in the evenings and I've given them all homework to use the gym at least twice a week between sessions. So many of the older players think they're gonna get picked automatically, but I keep telling Rhod that's not the way to do it any more. We have to reward commitment and fitness."

"You'll do fantastic this year, I know it. I'll buy a Pont scarf and hat and come to every match," I said. The young waitress came back with our food before Finn had a chance to reply. The steak in front of him was massive compared to my dainty little bit of fish, but I had full faith that he'd rise to the challenge.

"Bone apple-teeth," he said.

I laughed. "Funny, like the memes."

"Memes?" said Finn. "What...what's so funny about that?"

"Y'know, the memes. Bone-apple teeth, bone apple tea, boney m's feet..."

"So what you're saying is that people don't say bone apple teeth before food?" Finn looked genuinely confused, and I couldn't stop myself laughing. "I saw it on Facebook and

CHAPTER FIFTEEN - NATHAN

thought it was some French thing!"

"*Bon appetit* is the French," I replied through laughter. "Some guy misspelled it and got meme'd to hell."

"Oh my God," Finn buried his head in his hands. "I'm just gonna leave now. This is like when I said *weather foreskin* instead of *weather forecast* in front of the whole fucking Welsh team."

"You know what? I'm not even going to ask," I said. "I'll deal with language, you deal with rugby."

"Can you do the maths too?" Finn asked. "I'll take on gardening if you can do the maths."

"Sounds good to me, boyfriend." I held up my glass to clink against his. We each tucked into our food and somehow he was done with his massive fuck-off steak and chips before I'd made much of a dent in my salmon. I was aware of his eyes on me throughout every bite of my meal.

"Well that was delicious," he said once I was finished and rubbing my very round belly. "What's for dessert?"

"You have *got to* be kidding me," I said. No way could he eat a steak half the size of a cow and still be hungry. Finn called over the waitress with a raised hand. "Would you mind grabbing us a top up of these two sodas please? And a dessert menu if you have the time? Thank you darling."

The waitress nodded and I could see a blush creeping up her cheeks as she took our glasses up to the bar. "Do you even know the effect you have on people?" I asked him.

"Effect?" Finn looked even more puzzled than when he'd mangled French. "I have an effect?"

"You're big and tall, gorgeous and muscular, and you're friends with everyone the second you set eyes on them. I reckon that waitress would give you her number in seconds if you asked.

In fact, I bet she scribbles it on the receipt tonight."

"B-but I'm with you," Finn said. "Am I not making that obvious enough?"

I dropped my voice to a whisper. "Finn, we're not really together. I know this arrangement works for us, but if there is someone who you start to like, please don't hold back for me. I know you're a good guy with strong morals, but I can protect myself if needs be." I hated saying it. I knew why, at the back of my mind, but it was something I didn't want to admit out loud...or even to myself.

Finn blew out a breath and frowned. "You know I like you, right?" he whispered. "Like, this might all be fake, but I'm having a fucking fantastic time with you. And if I need to do anything to show more people that we are *together*, then I will. It's not just wanting to protect you. I genuinely care for you. So much."

I could feel my cheeks heat but worst of all I could feel tears pricking at the back of my eyes. I'd never had a relationship as real as this pretend one with Finn. And that hurt just as much as he made me feel happy.

The waitress came back over with the menu and drinks, and much as I'd predicted, there was a napkin folded on top of it.

"I'll leave you both to decide if there's anything extra you want," she said. Finn opened up the napkin then coughed and crumpled it and threw it into the centre of the table.

"Told you," I said, though I wasn't feeling all that smug. Why wouldn't he go for the pretty waitress?

"I can't believe this," he said. "Are you having dessert?"

"Nah, too full," I rubbed my belly. "Though if you're having something..."

"I'll allow you a bite," said Finn. "Finn don't share food."

CHAPTER FIFTEEN - NATHAN

He looked over bath the waitress, and waved her over again. Her smile faltered when Finn reached over the table to thread his big fingers through mine. "I'll have the chocolate fudge cake please. My boyfriend isn't too hungry but if you could bring an extra fork just in case he wants to share with me..."

He let the revelation hang in the air for a second. "Sure," said the waitress. "I'll be right back."

"She's so spitting in our food," I muttered.

"Let her," Finn said. "This relationship is real to the outside world until you think I've served my purpose, OK?"

"Until you've..." I didn't know what to say. It felt like we were on some kind of precipice, like if I said the right — or wrong — thing now I could send our relationship off in a whole different direction.

"What if we..." I started, unsure of where I was going next, when that *bloody* waitress arrived with Finn's chocolate fudge cake.

"Enjoy," she muttered then stalked back to the bar without checking if we wanted drink refills.

"She only brought us one fork," Finn muttered. He raised his hand to get her attention but she was looking studiously at a glass at the bar.

"You heartbreaker," I laughed.

"I didn't do anything!" Finn protested. "Fine, if she wants to play dirty, I'm playing dirtier."

He got a big chunk of fudge cake onto the fork and held it out toward me. "Want a bite?"

I reached for the fork, but Finn pulled it back. "Nope, open wide."

"You bastard," I whispered. I could feel myself grinning, and let Finn feed me the chocolate cake on the fork. "S'good," I mumbled through the chocolate cake in my mouth and Finn chuckled.

He looked over at the bar and back at me before having a bite. "She's looking," he confirmed.

There was a little bit of chocolate cake on his lip, so I reached over the table absently to swipe it off with my thumb. I heard a glass smash over at the bar.

"That wasn't even intentional!" I protested. We both looked over at one very red-faced waitress. "I promise!"

She was glowering, but it was someone else at the other side of the room my eyes were drawn to. My mother, normally the Iron Lady of the kitchen, was lounging against the wall and looking right at me, a smile playing at the corners of her mouth. "She likes you," I said to Finn.

"I know, that's why she's smashing things in the corner."

"No, my mother, stupid." I couldn't help but feel that we were somehow complicating things by bringing mothers into it now. But I was glad she liked Finn. I liked Finn. Everyone should like Finn.

"Right, shall I get the bill? My treat," said Finn.

"Well, technically it's Mum's treat. This is her apology for my dad forcing my company on you the other day I think."

"I can't do that! I liked having you there." Finn seemed to think for a second and stood up. "Wait here."

I watched as he stood up and went to talk to my mother. I couldn't hear what they were saying, but she was looking up at him and smiling in a way I hadn't seen her smile since I came back home. Finn took out his wallet and put a couple of notes in her hand, then turned to me with a grin and beckoned me to the exit.

I walked over to Mum and gave her a hug. "Thanks for tonight,

CHAPTER FIFTEEN - NATHAN

Mum. I really appreciate it."

"Well I'm glad you've found such a gentleman. He's welcome over whenever, no matter what your father says."

I headed over to where Finn stood at the door. "Would you like me to walk you home?" he asked.

"What a gentleman," I smiled. "What's to stop me walking *you* home?"

"Yours is closer, and I'm up at 6am for an early rugby session tomorrow," he said. "Otherwise I'd have you with me all night."

I took Finn's hand, because it felt natural, and we walked out of the Pont's car park and on to the road. We passed a group of men smoking, and I kept my firm grip on Finn's hand. Until one of them spoke, a voice I'd not heard in years.

"Nath? Is that you?" Lewis detached himself from the group of smokers. He looked older, much older than he had any right to in the few years we'd been separated. Under the street light I could see that he'd put on weight and there were lines on his face that I hadn't ever seen before. His hair was greying at the temples and his eyes were dull.

"Hi, Lewis," I muttered. He was swaying slightly. Still drunk then.

"I've...I've missed you," he said. I reached for Finn's hand again and gripped it harder than before. He'd been unusually silent for one so talkative and determined to protect me. It was time for me to use the fake boyfriend trick for it's intended purpose.

"Finn, this is Lewis, my ex," I started. "And Lewis, this is Finn. Finn is my-"

"Fiancé," Finn cut across, reaching out one hand to shake Lewis'. "Lovely to meet you."

Shit. Things had just gotten a lot more complicated.

16

Chapter Sixteen - Finn

The words had tumbled from my mouth before I could take them back. My brain, already not the fastest worker in any situation, had fumbled through a couple of options when I realised the bastard stood in front of me was the one who'd made Nathan so miserable for so long.

The options rushing through that thick skull had come so quickly I couldn't keep up. I could beat him into a pulp, which would be the most satisfying option and would see the bastard never look at Nathan again without remembering my fist crunching through his nose. I could intimidate him with words, which would maybe have the same effect. I had a good six inches of height on him as well as bulk and I bet he'd shit his pants if I so much as mentioned what I could do to him.

But I didn't do either of those things. Because Nathan didn't like men who did that kind of thing, and I never wanted him to be afraid of me. I never wanted him to see me use these fists to harm.

"Fiancé," I said. And watched two faces fall in unison. Lewis took an immediate step back, and I felt Nathan's grip on my

CHAPTER SIXTEEN - FINN

hand loosen. "So we'll just be on our way."

It wasn't until we were long out of sight and earshot of the smokers' group that Nathan wrenched his hand from mine and stalked ahead of us. "I cannot believe you, Finn!"

"What?" I was dumbfounded. "I just thought, out of all the things…"

Nathan was lit from above by one of the street lights, my beautiful little man like a light in the darkness of my life. And he was furious with me. "Why the fuck did you have to go and make this more complicated?

"I just…I didn't know what to say," I said honestly. "And I didn't want him in your head. I didn't want him able…able to hurt you."

"And you decided saying you were my fiancé was the best option?" Nathan asked. "The whole point of the *fake boyfriends* thing was to get that kind of thing off my back, to make my life a little easier, and to give you a cover. And you just complicated it all to hell, didn't you? All I had to do was introduce you as my boyfriend and that should've gotten him off my back.

"But…" I knew my excuse, and I knew it sounded pathetic. "I wanted it to sound more permanent."

"But we aren't permanent, are we? Much we might like that idea, just a little bit, this relationship is designed to fail once we've served our purpose to one another. And you just made breaking it off that much harder."

Nathan turned away and walked out of the light, towards home. And I knew I'd done wrong. I wanted to make sure he got home safe and sound, wanted to know that he was OK. But that wasn't the right thing to do, because Nathan needed me not to impose myself again. I'd fucked up. I'd fucked up bad.

I headed home slowly, willing myself not to cry. I managed

to keep the tears from falling until I finally made it inside. The fridge was fully stocked with beers and I had a nice couple of bottles of wine in the cupboard. I could get through the night.

* * *

My head was pounding. *Tap tap tap. Tap tap tap.* I tried to swat the noise away but failed. *Taptaptap. BANG BANG BANG.* Then I realised the source of the noise, and remembered why my head hurt. The collection of bottles on the table was indication enough of the head pain and I could see the shadow in the front door from my position laying on the carpet. I pushed myself up from the floor - I'd fallen asleep cradling a bottle of red wine which was now staining the carpet. If Nathan was behind the door and saw me like this...

What the hell. He knows I'm pathetic anyway. I headed for the door, unlocked the chain and opened it.

"Oh, hi, Rhod," I gestured him in. Despite the hangover pain in my head I was pretty sure I was still a little bit drunk.

Rhod looked up at me with disappointment in his eyes as he sidled past me and into the living room.

"Oh, fucking hell. What the fuck have you done, Finn?"

"Cuppa?" I offered. "Alexa, make me a coffee please. Double espresso, add some sugar. And some whiskey whilst you're at it." I swayed in place a bit and grabbed the sofa for support, suddenly worried I was going to be sick on it.

Rhod yanked on the curtains and I shielded myself from the sudden glare like a vampire. "What the *fuck*, Rhod? It's Saturday," I muttered.

"Yes, and you're the idiot missing the first friendly match

CHAPTER SIXTEEN - FINN

of the season because you've decided to drink yourself half to death," Rhod replied, The worst thing was the lack of anger in his voice. He sounded just as resigned to the situation as I was. I wanted him to be angry at me. Someone else needed to be.

"Bad night," I muttered as I tripped over the step into the kitchen to grab my coffee. My hand shook as I brought the mug to my lips and I managed to burn my tongue on the scalding hot coffee. "Shit."

"Shit indeed, young man. What has gotten into you?"

"Dunno. Don't care." I put the coffee down, and it sloshed over the counter. "Everything's just shit, isn't it."

"What's the problem?" Rhod asked. He looked so concerned that I felt sick.

"Why aren't you fucking *angry?*" I asked him. "Surely if you hated me half as much as I hate myself right now, you'd be screaming at me. Firing me. Telling me I'm a worthless piece of shit who doesn't deserve the trust you've given me."

"That was surprisingly eloquent, Finn. Grab a bin bag please." Rhod stepped into the living room and I had no choice but to follow, snagging a bag from a drawer on the way. I opened it on his instruction and stood silently as he dropped beer bottles and the wine bottle into it with a crash.

"The first time I had to deal with a young man who chose drink over a happy life, I was angry," said Rhod. "The second time, maybe the third, fourth, tenth times too. But I got over being angry at some point. And I got deeply, deeply sad. Because the living conditions here make people sad. The Welsh Valleys are crushed under the boot of whatever man or woman is in power. The jobs around here are terrible and life is *hard*. Most of us go to school, we become a plumber, or a shop assistant, or a cleaner, and we work until we're sixty-six. And then we die. Our fathers mined the coal in these valleys until their hands turned black and stopped working, and then they retired. And then they died. And that's the way it's been, forever. The Valleys are beautiful to an outsider. The green, green grass of home beckons you wherever you are. But these hillsides can be like a prison.

"And it drives a man to drink, it really does. You get angry, you drink, you get happy, you drink, you get sad, you drink. And then you die. Not necessarily from the drink, but you die a drinker. And people never, ever get out of the valley. Because they're too poor, or because their father drank, or because their mother drank and she beat their father black and blue for coming home from the pub late every single night. Rugby is an avenue away from all that for a lot of boys, Finn. It runs through our veins, it's in our blood and cuts us to the bone. No fancy doctor in Cardiff or lawyer in London puts their body on the line like a rugby player does. It gives purpose to someone who's got nothing but work. We drink after a game to celebrate, of course, but we get up in the morning, we go to work and we come home to our wives and our children, and the high of that life we've built for ourselves is enough for us to keep going."

Rhod paused for a minute, gathering up the bag before beckoning me to follow him into the kitchen. He opened the fridge and swept every single full bottle into the bag with a crash.

"Now you, Finn. You had it all. You had rugby, and you got out of this bastard valley like so few do. So no, I am not angry at you at all for falling back into drink. But it hurts me, it hurts my heart. I could never be angry at you. You boys are like my own children, and I have done my best to shepherd you all into being better. Into not drinking like all your fathers and their

CHAPTER SIXTEEN - FINN

fathers before them. So whatever has driven you back to this, I will do my best to help you get better."

The tears that had threatened to break free in the night were flowing now. "I don't deserve you, Rhod."

"No. You don't. Now, tell me what brought you back to this."

What could I say? I'd overstepped the fake relationship that Rhod very much believed was real, but I couldn't let him down for a second time today. So I just shook my head.

"Is it the job? Or being back here?" Rhod asked. I shook me head. "Is it your man?" I nodded slowly. "Damn, this is normally when I ask one of my players if he's gotten his girl pregnant, but I somehow don't think that's the case here."

I laughed through the tears, and wiped at my face with one wine-stained sleeve, the smell turning my stomach. "I..." I knew I had to stick to the truth as close as possible. " I pushed our relationship a bit further than he wanted to take it."

"You proposed?" Rhod asked. I nodded slowly. That was pretty accurate.

"And he said no?"

"Well..." I swept my hand across the room, gesturing at the wine stain on the carpet.

"Whatever was said or done, I'm sure your young lad likes you. Even if you've pushed a little too hard or fast. You're smart, you can work through it."

"Thanks, Rhod," I muttered. "Sorry about...everything."

"I said I wasn't angry , and I'm not. But you missed the first match for some of these boys today. It'll take a bit of work to make them know that you care, but I'm sure you can do it."

"Thank you." I pulled Rhod into a hug before he could protest. The world might have been swimming before me, my head might have felt like a strobe light was on a constant pulse inside, but I was going to be OK. I just had to get better. And part of that, once I'd given him the appropriate space, would be about apologising to Nathan.

"Right, I'm off to celebrate. You take today easy, but I want you in my office tomorrow to talk training for our first league game of the season. Some of the lads played shoddily in today's game, and that either because they didn't care that it was just a friendly or because they actually need more training, and we can talk about that then."

"Sure thing, Boss."

"Oh, one last thing," said Rhod, heading for the door. "I want you hosting an open session on Thursday evening after the regular training session. Maybe pick a player to help you? I'm sure we have some untapped gems in this valley."

"This valley mined coal, not diamond," I replied, feeling pretty damn slick.

"And what does coal turn into under pressure?" Rhod shot back before letting my door slam shut.

I was alone in the house. "I dunno, slightly harder coal?" I said to the empty room. And then I was running to the kitchen sink to throw up.

* * *

I was finally making progress on the wine-stain on the carpet when the door knocked again. I had spewed my guts up, showered, brushed my teeth and napped, and if I wasn't feeling fresh as a daisy then at least I was feeling a little fresher than before. I had opened the curtains and windows to let some air in and things were feeling OK.

I'd also found Rhod's wallet on my kitchen counter, so I was

CHAPTER SIXTEEN - FINN

sure the knocking on the front door was him. I picked it up from the coffee table, whistling as I opened the door. Not to the balding elderly gentleman who had known me since I was a kid, but to the pink-haired little guy who had become my world in a matter of weeks.

"Hi," I said awkwardly.

"Can I come in?" asked Nathan after a few seconds.

I stood aside to let him past me, knowing he'd see what I'd been up to. But in amongst all the lies to other people I knew this relationship needed to be built on honesty above all else.

"Busy morning then?" Nathan asked. I pulled off the marigold-yellow dish gloves I'd been wearing and moved the wash-bucket into the kitchen. The wine-stain was going to be a permanent addition to the cream floral carpet but I'd made a dent.

"...yeah," I confessed. "I was cleaning up after last night."

"Party? Have anyone round?" Nathan asked. The same tinge of jealousy in his voice that I knew would be in mine if I'd asked the question.

"No....just me," I said. "Would you...could you sit down? There's lot we need to talk about."

"I agree," said Nathan. "Alexa, coffee, make it fucking strong!"

I smiled at the fact he knew my house well enough now to shout at it. When I heard the coffee machine beep I brought the coffee in to him and sat on the arm of the seat to give him distance. Nathan took sip. "So. *Fiancé*."

"Fiancé," I replied. So we'd cover that first. "All I can say is...I'm sorry. I'm sorry to have put you in an awkward position, and I'm sorry to have said something so stupid...I just wanted to protect you without going all ape mode, and my stupid fucking brain came up with the worst possible solution to the problem."

"Sounds about right," said Nathan with a small smile. "I forgive you. But we're going to need to come up with a solution."

"Can't we just hope no one else finds out?"

"No one finds out what you blurted in the street in front of at least five drunk men, one of whom by all accounts has a habit of getting drunk and spouting off about me? Yeah, in this little village that'll go nowhere." Nathan laughed ruefully.

"We can say we broke up..." I suggested, barely managing not to wince.

"What if that's not what *I* want?" asked Nathan. "This is working out well for me at the moment, and it seems to me that if I want your company we're gonna have to keep up the ruse. I enjoy spending time with you Finn, it's just...that kinda fucked it all up."

"Then we're fake-engaged, for as long as you want us to be," I said. "You know those friends who say if they're not married by thirty-five they'll get married? Why not do it backwards? We're engaged now. And if you find someone you'd rather be with, we break off the engagement and pretend it never happened." I tried saying it as casually as I could. But it wasn't nice, the thought of breaking up with Nathan. Fake-breaking up. *Whatever.*

"That's the stupidest idea I've heard since *fake relationship*," said Nathan, and this time his smile seemed more genuine. "So naturally, I'm in."

"Great..." I said. "Though I want to be honest with you now, and if you want you can cut it all off."

"Well that only has me *slightly* worried," Nathan quipped.

"I have a problem with alcohol." I let it hang in the room

CHAPTER SIXTEEN - FINN

for a second before carrying on. "I don't think I've ever said that out loud before. But I had a problem before I left here for Cardiff and with fame and a bit of money it just got worse. I don't think I *needed* it every day, as such, but if there was a party with people getting drunk, I had to get the drunkest. If I wasn't sleeping through a hangover on a Sunday then there was no point to there being a Sunday. And at home, if I was alone by myself I'd polish off a crate of beer in a night."

Nathan didn't say anything, so I carried on. "I'm doing my best to get better, I promise. And Rhod gave me a real wake-up call today. My drunken behaviour fucked up my international career and I'm determined not to let it fuck up what little I have left. When I'm around you and I'm having a good time...it's easier not to drink. But I don't want it to be something that I need when I'm lonely. I want to be better. I need to be better."

Nathan put the cup of coffee down on the table and I wasn't sure if he was about to run out of the house and never look back. He launched himself at me and wrapped his arms around my neck. "I'm here for you, whenever you need to talk," he whispered in my ear. "I will be here as long you need me."

I cautiously let my arms wrap around Nathan to hold him close. His promise meant more to me than anything else in the world in that moment.

17

Chapter Seventeen - Finn

It was a warm evening, and the late summer sun had yet to set over the hillsides. Pont rugby club was getting a fresh coat of paint for the upcoming rugby season and our first game with Pandy was fast approaching. But Rhod had insisted that we start the open sessions for potential new players. I had the feeling he wanted to start a second, more inclusive team.

I had brought Ben along with me to help with our open rugby session. Rhod was right. We'd spent so long pushing at the current team, becoming an insular society that only accepted the best from the local high school, that we might have been missing out on some absolute gems in the community.

About twenty people had turned up for the open session, all between the ages of 16 and 30. Some had previous rugby experience, some had never touched a ball in their life. The goal of these open sessions was to get them comfortable with one another and the sport, and to build confidence. As Ben was pretty young and not the stereotypical rugby player with his gangly build, I hoped that he could encourage some enthusiasm and extract new or hidden confidence from the newbies.

CHAPTER SEVENTEEN - FINN

"Right then all, let's get started!" I shouted. "We'll start with a lap of the field!" There were groans from the group, but I needed to get an accurate measure of people's fitness before I could start telling them what they should and shouldn't be doing. Ben took the lead and the rest followed him as he shouted encouragement to them with cheesiness and overconfidence I hadn't felt since high school. As they all took off on a lap around the field - some, especially the younger ones were like rockets whilst some could manage a walk - I spotted a familiar flash of pink moving toward me across the field.

Fuck. It was a Thursday. Nathan's usual training day with me. He had started using the gym without me every now and then, but we still had a personal session every Thursday. And because I was disorganised enough to have never kept a diary in my life, I hadn't seen the potential clash. I could see Nathan's face, and his lips were turned down in a little frown that I wanted to wipe off his face.

I crossed the field toward him. "So, so sorry," I was already saying. "Rhod asked me to set all this up and I completely forgot and..."

Nathan reached out for my hand and grabbed it. "Don't worry, stupid. I get it. Pont comes first."

He didn't seem like he was pissed off in any way but I still felt fucking awful.

"I'll just head to the gym now...if it's still OK that I use it?" he asked. "Maybe I'll see you later then, when you're done?"

"Yeah...." I muttered. There was no solution to my idiocy, and Nathan would be left alone because of it. Nathan took a step away from me just as Ben skidded up next to us.

"Hey, you joining us for the session?" he asked.

Oh. There was the solution. So simple that even a hormonal, stupid teenager could see it. "Fancy giving rugby a go?" I asked Nathan.

"I don't know, I've never..." Nathan looked around, and seemed to notice that the people at the session weren't our *usual* lot. "Fuck it. Go on then."

"Everyone, this is Nathan...my...my Nathan. Be nice." I grinned at him and gestured for him to join the rest. "Lucky I'm not giving you an extra lap for lateness," I said.

"Lucky I'm not whooping your arse for being a shit personal trainer," he shot back. The whole group laughed. I smiled, and turned away so no-one could see that my eyes had gone a bit shiny. No-one could have predicted that the Nathan I met a month before would have built up the kind of confidence to get so cheeky in front of strangers.

"Right, for that kind of language, let's start the session with some fitness. I want to see where we're all at. Have any of you heard of the bleep test?"

There were more groans from the group. The schoolyard exercise - running between two sets of cones in time with a series of bleeps which got faster and faster, facing faster and faster runs - was a great measure of fitness, but bad experiences in PE had soured it for a lot of people. Ben had already set up the cones for me, and I had everyone line up for the first bleep to play from my phone.

There really were a range of fitness levels in the group. The first few started dropping out at around level four of the test, but I knew a few of them as heavy smokers and drinkers so I gave them a pat on the back as they left and flopped onto the grass. After that, there was a steady stream of dropouts until there were a few left, spearheaded by Ben. I was proud to see that my training regime had pushed him into getting so fit. I saw a lot of myself in his gangly frame and awkward gait.

And then there was Nathan. Huffing and puffing, but still going. Still pushing through at the same pace as the fittest. When he finally missed two beeps in a row and flopped onto the grass, I couldn't hold back my smile. Once Ben and the last of the guys dropped out. I let everyone have a drink and get their breath back.

"Now, for the rugby!" I said once almost everyone was standing. The air smelled of sweat and most were still panting and red-face but I could see a lot of smiles in the group. "We've not got much time tonight but I thought we'd have a bit of fun. Next week we'll focus on ball skills and passing practice, if I haven't scared you all off this week with fitness. But today Ben has gotten the tackle pads out. Ben's going to show you all how to tackle. We want it low, below the shoulder. And you wrap your arms around your target to bring them down."

I held up the heavy foam tackle pad and Ben moved in in an exaggerated slow movement, pushing his one shoulder against the pad and wrapping his arms around it. He stepped back and repeated the action again and again, faster each time until he was pushing me back with a grunt. The kid was getting surprisingly strong.

"Right, pair up. Grab a tackle pad each pair. The goal is *not* to tackle your opponent to the ground, it's to practice the technique."

I watched as the group paired up. I didn't like that Nathan paired up immediately with one of the biggest guys there, but Ben grabbed my elbow as I stepped forward to move them around. "You wouldn't stop me doing it, so don't stop him."

"When did you get so fucking smart?" I asked.

"When you got so fucking dumb," Ben replied.

"For that, you're cleaning out the showers late," I said.

"Nope, I've got a date with my girlfriend...and her girlfriend," Ben grinned.

"Bloody hell, Ben. You've got two girlfriends now?"

"No, I have a girlfriend, and my girlfriend has a girlfriend. We don't all date each other, we're both dating...anyway, doesn't matter. We're all meeting together for the first time tonight."

"Well...be safe," is all I could think to say. I may not understand it, but there was no way I was going to get in the way of it. I'd heard too many stories of valleys kids getting shunned by their parents to be the judgemental older figure in Ben's life.

We watched as the pairs of lads practised tackling, and Nathan was obviously taking his much bigger opponent by surprise, Every run and wrap performed by Nathan pushed back the bigger guy by a couple of inches. My man— my fake man, anyway — could take on the world.

When I called for them to swap, I watched the group like a hawk. I didn't like the angry look the bigger guy was giving Nathan. He was a big bastard, and obviously wasn't used to getting pushed round by someone six inches shorter and half his height. Rugby was great for getting aggression out in a safe environment. I was just watching to make sure he didn't do anything too stupid.

The second the tackle pad was in Nathan's hands, the big guy took a run forward and smashed it — and Nathan — into the hard ground. I was moving toward the two of them before Ben could stop me.

18

Chapter Eighteen - Nathan

The breath had been knocked out of me, and I laid looking up at the sky for a minute as I fought to get it back. I smiled despite it though. Playing rugby, getting roughed up...it was an exhilarating experience despite the aches and bruises. I'd paired up with Carl, the biggest guy there, because he had smiled shyly and said he'd never played rugby before so despite the size difference he seemed like the best option.

So when I finally realised what was going on around me, it was a shock to say the least. Finn was over me, his hands bunched up in Carl's t-shirt, and he was shouting something at him.

"Woah, woah. What's going on?" I asked. They both looked down at me like they'd forgotten I was there.

"He hurt you!" Finn said.

"And I told Carl to give me his all," I said. "I just hadn't realised how much *his all* was. So back up, big boy."

"Oh." Finn's hand loosened, and Carl took a step back. "Sorry...Carl."

I held up a hand and Carl helped me up. "Sorry, mate," he said.

"No harm, no foul," I said. "Finn's been toughening me up. In a couple of weeks, I'll be able to do the same to you."

Carl laughed and held his hand up for a high-five. It was odd how easy it was being around someone like him now. Finn had reminded me that not all big valleys men were utter bastards.

Finn looked between us like he didn't know what to do, before turning to the group at large. "Right then boys, that's us done for the day! I'll clear up, you get clean."

As one, everyone turned to walk over the field to the changing rooms. I hesitated for a second, then ran to get my training bag from the sidelines and followed them. "See you later?" I asked Finn. He nodded.

By the time I'd caught up with everyone, some people were already in the showers and others were stripping out of their training clothes. I had showered a couple of times with Finn now, and things weren't so awkward any more. The laddish banter put me at ease more than it scared me now, so I stripped down and joined them in the shower.

"Sorry again," said Carl. "I forgot how strong I was. My fiancé will kill me if she hears I got too rough in training."

"Seriously mate, it was no issue. Don't panic. Finn is just overprotective."

"If someone knocked over my fiancé like that, I'd have him by the scruff of the neck too," said Carl. "So I get it. Finn really loves you."

"Oh," was all I could think to say. I knew Finn was my best friend in Pontycae. But did he *love* me or was he just so overprotective with all his friends? Then again, his friends for the most part were Carl's size or bigger. Maybe he didn't need to be.

I followed Carl out of the shower and to the benches and we

CHAPTER EIGHTEEN - NATHAN

kept talking as we changed. He told me how he'd proposed to his girlfriend over Christmas, their plans for the wedding in Pont's church and how much they wanted two kids and three dogs. I hadn't realised until I shoved my glasses over my nose that the rest of the changing room had cleared out.

"You coming back next week?" he asked.

"I think I will, yeah. If Finn hasn't wrapped me up in cotton wool by then."

Carl laughed as the door swung open, and Finn was stood in the doorway, Once again, his expression was completely inscrutable. "See you next week then," said Carl, cuffing me on the shoulder before he left.

Finn stood in the doorway for a long moment, before sinking to his knees on the tiled floor in front of me. "Are you OK?" he asked. Hi hands roamed my body as if searching for wounds and I did my best not to blush as he touched my skin.

"I'm *fine*, Finn. You don't have to go all caveman. Remember, you've wanted me to be able to stand up for myself. I'm doing that. If I ever want you to stand in a fight for me, I'll ask."

"You're right," he said. "And I am so, so proud of you."

"As you should be," I winked. Seized by the impulse, I leaned forward to kiss him. I coasted fingers through his close-cropped hair. He kissed me back fervently, his hands finding their way under my shirt.

I hadn't buckled my belt yet so Finn fumbled with my zipper. "No one should be coming in any time soon," he said. "Is this OK?"

"Yeah," I said, leaning in to kiss him again as his hand brushed over my boxers and my hardening cock straining against them. Finn's big hand fumbled with my waistband before pulling my cock free. Already on his knees, he dipped his head down and licked a strip up the length. I shuddered, laying back against the cold tiled wall. Finn took the head of my cock in between warm lips and then sank down its length in one quick motion. It felt amazing, having his lips on me and to be the focus of an act I'd always been expected to do myself.

And then the doubt started to set in. Were the moans Finn was making at the back of his throat pleasure, or some kind of performative obligation like I'd done so many time? Surely he didn't *like* servicing me with nothing in return, I'd never liked all that. And what if someone did walk in? Fuck, Finn would lose his job. And I'd-

"Hey, sweetie. Where'd you go?" Finn was still on his knees in front of me, hands rubbing my thighs and lips withdrawn from my slightly softening cock.

"Nothing, uh, nowhere. Just..." I reached for Finn's face and he rose to meet me for a gentle kiss. With shaking hands, I fumbled for his belt. If I couldn't stay hard for him then I could at least return the favour, make the effort worthwhile for him.

"Woah, woah." Finn pulled back from the kiss. "I can see your mind went elsewhere, you're not in the mood for this."

"No, I can..." but Finn was already gently tucking me away and zipping up the front of my jeans.

"C'mon, Nath." He took my hand, which I hadn't realised was still shaking so much, and he grabbed my bag with all of my workout gear in it too. "Let's get you some place safe."

"Seriously Finn, if you want it, I can do it." I was trying to assert myself. Had I failed? All I had to do was enjoy a *fucking* blowjob but my mind just wasn't letting me get past some kind of mental block.

"Teenage sex education has a lot to fucking answer for," said Finn. "When you're ready, we're going to go back to my house

CHAPTER EIGHTEEN - NATHAN

and have a cup of tea, OK?"

We walked silently, hand in hand except for when Finn had to lock up the training centre. But he held my hand across the field, through the streets of Pontycae, and all the way to his home. Finn sat me down in his living room on a sofa that was feeling increasingly familiar, and went into the kitchen.

"Would you like a cup of tea?" he asked.

"Yes please?" I answered, more of a question than an answer. He'd already told me we would be coming back to his house and we'd be having tea. Why ask again?

After couple of minutes, Finn walked into the living room holding tow big steaming mugs. "Would you still like this cup of tea?" he asked.

"Yes please," I said. Finn placed the mug down in front of me.

"Just so you know, I'm not the best tea-maker in the world. If you pick up the cup of tea and then put it down, and drink none of it, I won't be offended. If you drink half and then decide you've had too much, I won't take offence. Even if you drink it down to the very last dregs and decide you're too full, you shouldn't feel obligated to finish." Finn took a particularly loud slurp of his own tea.

"I feel like you're trying to make a point here that I'm too stupid to understand," I said. I reached for my cup of tea and took a sip. "Though this is not a bad cup of tea, so if it is just general insecurity over your ability to boil a kettle I think we can settle that."

"When I was younger, I was what the lads would call a *top shagger*," said Finn. "I got with girls pretty openly and lads secretly, and everyone knew I was fucking up for it. If you wanted to fuck, I would pretty much always be up for it. And that was OK. Until it wasn't. And there were times I was just fucking for the sake of it, long after I'd stopped enjoying it. Or in stupid places."

Finn's words sounded familiar. I knew the feeling, that rush of being with Lewis, that excitement that things were going to happen and then the feeling that things weren't going quite right. That I should have been enjoying things more than I was because I was getting what I'd wanted, so I put up and shut up.

Finn continued. "When I finally joined Cardiff, I was doing the same with a much bigger pool of people. I lost count of the amount of people I'd had sex with because it was there and available and why wouldn't I just take the opportunity? And then a player up in Leicester got caught up in a sexual assault case and the rugby union made all the teams show their players some stupid video on consent. Or at least I thought it was stupid. Consent is simple, two people want to fuck, they say that's what they want, then you just go in-out-in-out til it's over."

"Right," I said. "Still no idea where this is going."

"Well the video was about cups of tea, and how they're like sex."

"Better than sex, sometimes," I muttered, and Finn smiled.

"Well, you know you can put a cup of tea down at any time. Even if you've said you'll drink it. You can stop drinking and come back to it, or you can stop altogether. There is no point where it's not OK to put the cuppa down. And it's the same with sex. Just because you've said yes at the start isn't a commitment to keep going until the end."

"But..." I didn't know what exactly I was going to say next. It felt like something in my world view had shifted.

"I know, I spent like a week going over it all in my head," said Finn. "It's a crazy thought, that actually maybe all those things

CHAPTER EIGHTEEN - NATHAN

I was doing out of a sense of obligation weren't healthy."

"So..." I said, "there were times when I was having sex with Lewis, and I'd kinda enjoy it early on, but then things would get painful. It always felt like I should..."

"Just grin and bear it? I know," said Finn. "I looked back and realised the amount of times I'd carried on past the point of caring, or had sex when I was too drunk to really enjoy it..." he trailed off, and I could see that despite how he'd helped me he was now deep in his own thoughts.

"Can I...can I have a hug?" I asked. " I just think I need to be held."

Finn put down the mug and held out his arms. I shuffled my butt across the sofa and onto his lap. Warm arms held me, and I leaned onto his chest. I felt safe, warm and...loved. I didn't know what kind of love, but I felt loved.

"Thank you," I said, "for teaching me that. I think I knew. I can blame Lewis for lots of things, but I don't think either of us understood what we were doing when it came to consent."

"Do you feel sorry for him?" Finn asked.

"I do pity him now," I said. "I've been thinking on it. It's weird how scared I felt of him when I first moved back. I think he's suffered the same upbringing we all did here, and his parents weren't nearly as lovely as mine. I can't imagine..."

"How did things end?" Finn asked abruptly.

I hesitated. I had never told anyone about this. *This* was what had scared me about coming back home, and why I'd been so fucking terrified the first day when I'd seen Charlie and Ryan in the pub, before my knight in shining armour had insisted he was my boyfriend.

"So when I went off to uni and Lewis stayed here, it already felt like a little rift, y'know? I was leaving the valley and going to Cardiff and he was staying here. I think he felt a bit at a loss, to have been forced out of the closet the way he was and then to be in a long distance relationship. But we...made it work. He'd come to Cardiff every now and then, and I would come home to see my parents. We weren't a million miles away but it felt like it sometimes, in terms of where we were mentally. I was studying at university and he was working behind the bar at the rugby club like he had when he was sixteen.

"Then one day I came home early, and he wasn't home or in work. I knew he liked to walk in the woods where we...where we had done stuff before. So I thought I'd go looking for him. And I found him. On his knees in front of one of the other boys from the rugby team."

"So all of that time, where he hadn't touched you, and used you, he was doing all that for someone else?" Finn asked. I could see him connecting the dots in his mind, and his arms tightened around me.

"Not quite," I said. "I found out later, when he was crying and begging, that nothing happened until I'd already left. But he said he wasn't doing all that to me because of...essentially, I wasn't man enough. Like we were in some hierarchy where he did that stuff for the bigger, stronger man because he was bigger and manlier, and then I was at the bottom of the pile, being used by him. Like if I found some femboy twink even smaller than me then I could make him as miserable as Lewis had made me."

"You don't still believe all that do you?" Finn asked. "That you being a little less macho means you have to serve?"

I could feel blush coming, borne more of embarrassment than anything else. I wanted to say *no, I don't believe any oof that any more.* But I couldn't. Because I did believe that, deep down.

CHAPTER EIGHTEEN - NATHAN

"Imagine me fucking you Finn, and tell me you don't think that's ridiculous."

"I don't." Finn took my hand in his and kissed my palm. "Most people have put me in this big *top* box because I'm built like a brick shithouse and the size of...well, you know. But I'd love to switch things up a bit. Bottom."

"Yeah, but not for me..." I could have laughed. How weird did that sound? It'd be like a chihuahua humping a Great Dane if I tried it with Finn.

"If you are a bottom, then fine. But tell me honestly, if we could fuck — with no judgement, no fear of it going wrong, and my promise to you that I will never push you beyond what's comfortable...would you?"

"What if I do it wrong, though?" I asked. "What if I get so into it that I forget..." I didn't know how to carry on.

"You're worried that you'll end up like Lewis?" Finn asked. I nodded. "And you don't think that you worrying about being like that pretty much confirms you never will be?"

"And you promise you'll tell me if you're uncomfortable or something feels wrong?" I asked him. I hadn't realised I'd been tangling my fingers in the front of his t-shirt.

"Promise," said Finn. "It feels so right, though." And then he was kissing me even as he stood and carried me up the stairs in a bridal lift, like it was so easy for him. He placed me gently down on his bed. "So long as you promise to do the same for me."

"Promise," I parroted.

Finn laid down on the bed next to me and kissed me gently. One finger hooked under my t-shirt. "Can I take this off?" he asked.

I nodded, and Finn pulled off my t-shirt and threw it to the floor. He kissed me, then moved down to my neck, my collarbone, then to my chest. He worshipped my body slowly and gently and took every moan and undignified squeak from my mouth as consent. Knowing I could stop at any point made it so much easier to carry on. Knowing the respect, as well as the reverence for me with which Finn dragged his stubbled chin over my smooth skin, made the whole experience that much better.

Finn bit at the waistband of my boxer-briefs that peeked over my trousers and looked up at me. My cock was straining underneath my jeans, but he was hesitating. For me.

"Please," I muttered to him. "Just do it."

Without speaking, Finn unbuttoned my jeans and peeled them back from my waist, then pulled at my underwear with them until they were both on the floor and my cock was free. He took my cock in his big hand and licked gently at the head.

"You fucking tease," I said, bucking in his hand at every swipe of his tongue. Finn grinned and took me in his mouth, taking it right to the back of his throat like I'd never interrupted us earlier in the changing room. He hummed around my cock and it felt like the vibrations travelled through my whole body.

I felt so overwhelmed, like I was coming out of my skin. It was good, but...I tapped Finn on the shoulder and he looked up, then came up off my cock with a little *pop* of suction that made me giggle. I gestured for him to come back up the bed and he crawled up to draw level with me. "Everything OK?" he asked.

"Yeah. I just...." Unsure of how to continue, I kissed him again, then broke the kiss to take his t-shirt off. I trailed fingers through the carpet of dark hair on his chest and he shuddered.

"I can trim all this back again if you like, I used to be smooth from my neck to my balls," Finn said.

CHAPTER EIGHTEEN - NATHAN

I laughed. "I like it, I've told you that," I said, dipping my fingers under his waistband to feel the forest of fur there too. "Can you...can you sit on the edge of the bed? And take these off?"

Finn silently moved over to the bed. I knelt on the floor in front of him. He angled his hips upward to pull off his tracksuit bottoms and his underwear and his massive cock sprang free. I took it in my hand, thumb and forefinger straining to meet around it. I moved my hand up and down, pulling the foreskin back from the head and then back over it. A little bead of precum gathered at the tip, and I swiped my finger over it to make him groan before I slowly, hesitantly lowered my mouth to the tip.

19

Chapter Nineteen - Finn

Nathan's lips at the very tip of my cock were heaven, and I was hard as an iron rod in his hand. He gently and teasingly nipped and licked at the head, drawing more precum out with every swipe of his tongue or gentle suck. He wasn't trying to take any more of me, but I could handle that. I was happy to let Nathan take things at his own pace, even if that meant I had to use a superhuman amount of effort not to buck up into his mouth. He had a mouth I could own if he would let me. But I wanted him to want it all as much as I did.

His hand was shaking as he milked yet more of my pre-release before licking a stripe up the underside of my cock right up the sensitive link between my foreskin and the head. "Are you OK with this? You're shaking," I double checked.

Nathan nodded and gave a shaky smile. "Yes, Finn. It's not fear, it's excitement."

He put his lips back to the head of my cock and slid his mouth down further, gagging before he got halfway. But he moved back up and tried again, getting slightly further. He had no chance of deep-throating me on the first try, but he used his hand to stroke the base of my cock as he used his mouth to stimulate the head and top of the shaft. My fists were bunched up in the sheets with the effort of not moving my hips and letting him do things his way.

Nathan kissed the head of my cock and then peppered kisses down my shaft and over my balls. I laughed and at the same time had a whole body shudder as his nose nuzzled over my sac. "Fuck, you're killing me, Nath," I said.

Nathan didn't say anything, just insistently pushed at my thighs until they were above my head and he'd exposed my ass over the edge of the bed. I looked up to the ceiling, and felt his thumbs spreading my cheeks.

"I swear, I can trim more down there if you think it's gross…" I started to say, but was cut off by the warm, wet feeling of Nathan's tongue swiping across my hole. "Fucking hell," I gasped. I'd never had this done to me before — I'd never done it to anyone else, either, with how quick and impersonal my fucks had been. But Nathan was lapping at my hole like he was born to do it, and I moved my hands from the bedsheets to grip at the back of my thighs, to give him more access if he needed it.

Nathan's tongue was no longer just a flat pad over my hole. He was alternating those bigger licks with more daring entrances. He tongue-fucked me and all I could do was watch my cock leaking precum into my forest of stomach hair, twitching with neglect. I knew a couple of strokes and I'd be done, if Nathan let me. And I wanted him to know he was completely in control. His tongue was replaced by a probing finger that gently pushed into me, opening me up. Then there were two, and I hissed as they entered too quickly.

"Fuck, sorry!" Nathan had stood up, and I had to laugh at the look of concern on his face even as he was completely naked and his dick standing at attention. "Was that too much? I never want it to be too much."

"Calm down, tiger," I said, reaching over my head to the bedside drawer. I threw the lube and condom down on the bed. "Try that out."

Nathan gave me a shy smile. He didn't kneel down at the edge of the bed now, he stayed stood up as he dripped some lube from the bottle directly onto my taint, and then pushed it into my hole with one finger. I could tell now he was watching my expression carefully for enjoyment, so I gave him a smile. I was focusing on opening up for him, and it had been so long since I had had to. Nathan might have been a smaller guy, but he certainly wasn't small in proportion.

More lube on my hole, and a second finger was pushing in much easier than it had with Nathan's spit for lube. I groaned as his two fingers found my prostate, and lost grip of my thighs for a second as it felt like my whole body loosened up. My cock was still dripping onto my stomach, and Nathan was looking down with so much concentration he may as well have been studying for an exam.

"Relax," I groaned at him. "You're doing...oh fuck...so good."

Nathan's fingers retreated and then he was holding up the condom. "Do you really want me to?" he asked.

"As long as you want to," I said. "I want whatever you'll give me."

I watched as Nathan rolled on the condom and slicked himself up with the lube. I grabbed the pillow from the end of the bed and pushed it under my arse so he wouldn't have to crouch so much, and he flashed a shaky but grateful smile. He grabbed my legs again so that my ankles rested on his shoulders, then

CHAPTER NINETEEN - FINN

notched his cock at my entrance where I hung over the bed. This was happening. It was really happening.

Nathan pushed in slowly, his hands gripping my calves to keep them high. I breathed out as I adjusted to the feeling of him inside me. Nathan was so slow, so careful, that I wanted to grip his arse and pull him into me faster. But again, I let him take it at his pace. And when he was finally seated deep inside me, I wanted to fucking cheer.

Nathan pulled back and pushed back in, and the upward curve of his cock brushed against my prostate inside me and made me moan. My cock twitched on my stomach. "Fuck me hard, Nath."

"Yeah?" asked Nathan. Still so unsure.

"Yeah. I need this. I need you," I said. "Just please, please, fuck me hard."

Nathan pulled back and pushed in again, harder this time so that I could hear the slap of skin as our bodies clashed. He started pumping harder and harder into me, and pushed my legs further back over my chest and he leaned forward for a better angle. Every thrust made me moan at an octave I don't even know my voice could fucking hit, and Nathan's smile was sure, confident now as he pulled those moans from me with expertise. This man had never topped? I didn't fucking believe it.

Nathan was too short to kiss me, but he'd pushed my legs right back toward my chest. He licked a stripe up one of my feet and I shuddered, which made him grin even more. I couldn't believe that he was getting so confident so quickly. Nathan reached around my leg to grip my cock.

"No, gonna...gonna cum," I said, trying to stop him from finishing me off well before he could finish.

"Me too," Nathan whispered, taking a firmer grip on my cock and stroking up and down as he pounded faster into me.

"Fuuuuck," I could feel my balls tightening as my orgasm built, and then I was spilling all over Nathan's hand and onto my stomach. I was cumming like I hadn't released in weeks, and it was coating my stomach. Nathan's hand moved from my cock to my stomach and his hand smeared the cum through my stomach hair. He moaned, low and long, as he thrust a couple more times and then buried himself to the hilt in my arse.

"Yes, Finn," he muttered, stilling as he came. After a couple of seconds, he pulled out and tied off the condom. And looked down at me, the mess he'd made on my stomach, and laughed.

I laughed too, because it was fucking wonderful to see Nathan — who'd told me all of the shit he'd gone through, all his hang-ups over sex — so *joyful.* I eased myself up into a sitting position, wincing as I put more weight on my arse, and then stood up to hug Nathan, not caring about all the stickiness between us.

"Was that OK?" he asked.

"More than OK," I said. "It was...." Mind blowing, amazing, the most intimate sex I'd ever had? "It was great, Nath. You were great."

"Thanks Finn. For everything." Nathan's voice was muffled against my chest. He pulled away from me with a gross squelch, and we both laughed again.

"Shower?" I asked. Nathan nodded, but then his phone was ringing.

He picked up. "Now? Really, Dad? What do you..." he put down the phone and looked at me. "Dad needs me, but he won't say for what. And Mum is in work." He looked around for a second, his eyes landing on the pile of clothes on the floor, then more frantically as he wiped off a hand on his own body.

"There's towels in the chest of drawers," I said. Nathan turned, and I realised my mistake as he did.

"What are those there for?" he asked, pointing at the big bunch of rings I'd left laying around on top of the chest of drawers. I could lie, I knew — tell him I'd just found them or forgotten they were there. But lying to Nathan went against my core.

"I, uh...after the whole proposal thing, I looked through my Gran's old rings. In case you wanted to carry on with the illusion. I dunno, maybe it was stupid."

"Not stupid, thoughtful," said Nathan, picking one plain gold band up and slipping it on to his finger. It fit perfectly. "Just don't tell anyone we've been living in sin."

And when he smiled again, like he hadn't stopped smiling at me all night, I knew I was a goner for him.

20

Chapter Twenty - Nathan

Going home after a night with Finn was like one of his ice baths after a workout — unpleasant but a necessary evil. I'd been neglecting my business a bit and leaving my poor mum to deal with my father more than I should have, and now he needed me. Finn was like an oasis in the desert, but I couldn't stay with him forever. I just got to go back and take cool sips of water when I really needed to, to keep me sane. The ring was a heavy reminder on my finger that I was living between these two worlds, the balance frail.

The house was quiet as I opened the door, but after a couple of seconds I could hear my father groaning and swearing from the kitchen. I rolled my eyes, closed the front door and went to see what the problem was with him.

I entered the kitchen quietly. Dad was wrestling with a jar of pickled eggs and still swearing under his breath.

"Need some help?" I asked.

Dad jumped — as much as a man in a wheelchair could — when he noticed me, and dropped the jar onto the tiled floor. It smashed, and glass and eggs went everywhere. "For fuck's

CHAPTER TWENTY - NATHAN

sake!" he shouted. "That's your fault!"

"Sure it is, Dad." I headed to the utility room to grab the sweeping brush, paper towels and the strongest kitchen cleaner I could find. Mum would go *ape* if she got home and the whole place smelled like a pickling factory.

"Come on Dad, shift back," I said. He was still sat in the middle of the kitchen like he'd frozen. There was pickle juice splattered up his pyjama trousers, and the juice was pooling around his wheels. I helped him gently move back. The wheels of his chair crunched over some glass, and I winced thinking of the scratches on the expensive tiled floor.

I swept up the broken glass and eggs without speaking, dumped them in an empty bin bag and then got to my hands and knees to clean up the pickling juice all over the floor.

"You should be focusing on helping me, not the fucking floor," Dad muttered. "I'm soaked."

"Unlike you, the floor has no capacity to clean itself," I replied. He stopped grumbling for a second so I sprayed as much of the nice-smelling spray on the floor and mopped up all the pickle juice. As I swiped the kitchen towel into the corner of the room I felt a sharp sting of pain. "Fuck!"

I pulled out the little shard of glass from my finger and threw it into the bin bag with the rest of the crap from the kitchen floor. "Ow, fuck!" I said again. The pain was only getting worse from the potent combination of pickle juice and cleaning product on the floor that must have mixed into the wound. I ran it under the cold water of the tap for a minute until it ran clear, then wrapped it up in a paper towel.

"Are you OK?" Dad asked hesitantly.

"Like you care," I shot back.

"I...I do care," he said. "Not always in the way you expect me to, but I do care for you."

"You've wanted me gone from the second I came home, Dad. You've done nothing but demand more help from Mum and I than we can give and you've done everything you can to make me uncomfortable. I would do anything for you, and I know there was a time you'd have done anything for me too. But it seems cruel, the way you treat me and Mum now. God knows I don't know how it feels to lose a leg but I know how depression feels, and you're dragging everyone else into it with you. You've had the whole house adapted to suit you, but you would rather sit there and complain that you're covered in shit than wipe it off yourself. You've disrespected my business, my relationship, and you have made me feel uncomfortable in this place that once felt like home."

"I..." Dad started, but a gentle cough made both of us jump. Mum was stood in the doorway and looking between us like she'd been watching a tennis match.

"Oh, bless you Noel. How did you manage to do that to yourself? Let's get you to the shower." Mum was across the kitchen in seconds and wheeling him out into the downstairs wet room. I wondered how much of my rant she'd heard. And how much she agreed with. For fuck's sake, he couldn't even open a jar any more because he'd let muscles go to waste.

I mopped up the tracks of brine that the wheelchair had made through the kitchen then ran up to the upstairs shower to get the smell off me. It had been a long day, and I was sad that Finn's hoodie was covered in the gross smell. I'd have to give it back to him after a wash and then take it back.

It was so easy to think of Finn as my boyfriend and for all intents and purposes, he was acting like one. I'd never fucked outside of a relationship, I'd never been one to hold hands in

CHAPTER TWENTY - NATHAN

the street. I'd never been one to...I looked down at the beautiful ring on my finger. If Finn hadn't opened his bloody mouth and made up the fake-fiancé lie, it would be a hell of a lot easier to move this relationship into something real.

I showered off the gross sulphury smell and threw all my clothes into the wash, changed into my pyjamas — TARDIS print — then headed downstairs. I was determined that I would talk with my father, even if Mum was too scared to rock the boat.

When I got downstairs I could hear the TV. The living room lights were dimmed, Dad was snoring on one sofa in his dressing gown, and Mum was sipping from a glass of red wine.

"Don't wake him," she whispered, then gestured out towards the kitchen. I headed out and she followed me a few seconds later, pulling the door closed behind her so that we wouldn't be heard.

"Wine?" she asked, grabbing a bottle from the fridge. I shook my head so she grabbed the carton of orange juice and poured me a glass of that instead, and topped up her own wine.

We sat in silence for a couple of minutes, and she had almost finished her new glass of wine before she spoke. "You know he's not a bad man, Nathan. I know that too."

"We went over this before Mum. He's acting like a bad man, whether you think he is one or not. He is not acting like a man who loves either of us right now."

"I know, but this has been hard for him...."

"God, Mum! Can't you see he's trying to push us away?" I said, coming to that same realisation at the same time as I said it. "God, I'm so stupid. He's trying to *push us away*."

"What do you mean? All he's done so far is beg for my help with every little thing."

"Exactly, and it's making you resent him. Be honest, it is, isn't it?"

Mum nodded slowly. When she took another gulp of her wine I continued. "When...everything happened with Lewis, I didn't just run away from Pontycae. I pushed everyone away. And I think that's what Dad is doing. He hates himself so much for what's happened, that rather than accept our help he'd rather push us to break. To leave him. So he doesn't inflict that misery on anyone else."

"I remember calling you and getting one word texts back," said Mum. "I felt like you were blaming us for not protecting you enough from...everything."

"No, Mum. I moved away and did my best to push you all away because I felt helpless. I was angry, at Lewis and myself, for the situation we'd gotten ourselves into. And I was angry with myself for being so weak. I didn't want your love or help because that would make me weak."

Mum sat silent for a minute. Then she put the glass down on the counter and walked around the kitchen counter and squeezed me tight. Her head rested on my shoulder. I realised we hadn't hugged in the entire time I'd been back. "We did fail you, Nath," she said. I felt my shoulder getting warm and damp and realised she was crying into my t-shirt. "Your father and I weren't enough to keep the bad at bay. I wish we'd protected you better."

"Mum..." I didn't know what to say. Thankfully, I didn't have to. Because she screamed loud enough to wake up the whole street, let alone my father in the living room.

I whirled around, expecting an assassin at the kitchen door or at the very least a massive fuck-off spider. But Mum had clutched my hand and was looking down at the lovely gold ring

CHAPTER TWENTY - NATHAN

that Finn had slipped on to my finger. "What the hell is that?" she breathed.

"Oh. Right. Uh," I managed. "Thing is..."

I didn't know if it was the emotional chat we'd already had or the need to tell *someone* who didn't live in another village 90 miles away what had been going on, but I spilled everything to Mum then. The fake relationship, the idiotic decision that Finn had made in front of Lewis.

"But...you're real now, right?" Mum asked. "Because at the restaurant there was nothing false about the way you looked at one another."

"God knows, Mum." I held up my left hand. "This thing just complicated things to another level. If we do make it official, then we're definitely not engaged. But eventually it'll get out that we *were* and then suddenly we're not..."

"He's a nice man, Nathan," Mum interrupted. "All I ever wanted for you, especially after Lewis, was that you found someone *nice.* Do you think a little complication like that should get in the way of your relationship?"

"A little? Mum, a man who was pretending to be in a relationship with me told someone he was my fiancé! How is that a little complication?"

"And yet I doubt he forced that ring onto your finger, did he?"

"...no." I reached for the orange juice and took a swig. "The strong stuff. That hits the spot."

Mum laughed. "Well, you're a big boy. I can't tell you what to do any more. All I can do is say that he's nice, and I'm glad that there's someone out there who treats you like you deserve to be treated."

"Thanks, Mum." My phone buzzed in my pocket. "Oh, speak of the devil..."

The smile slipped off my face as I realised it wasn't Finn trying to get into contact with me, but the actual Devil.

Lewis: Can we talk?

21

Chapter Twenty-One - Finn

It was game day. And I knew, in the grand scheme of things, that a non-league friendly game against a team that was technically a league below was not exactly the highlight of the rugby season. But the game between Pont and Pandy was a legendary yearly event in the village of Pontycae. And half my team weren't *fucking here*.

OK, we still had an hour to go until game-time. And some of the lads had begged off with a stomach bug that seemed to be doing the rounds. I should have been seeing a whole team of fifteen plus eight subs in case of injury. Instead I was facing seventeen players altogether. It was pathetic, and in a game against Pandy, we would need all the injury cover we could get. I left the boys chatting in the changing room and headed in to Rhod's office, where he was sat behind the desk scribbling some play tactics down like I hadn't already run through and decided what we were going to do.

"This is fucking dire," I said to him. He looked up from his pad and paper and gave me a grim smile, the same kind of ridiculous Valleys smile he'd given whenever a player had broken a leg on the field. So I knew behind that smile lay the same worry I was feeling.

"Rugby is dying in these hillsides," he said. "It's up to us to revive it, I told you that. The fact we can field a whole playing team is an achievement compared to some other teams."

"You don't fucking mean that though do you?" I said, my voice going up an octave with the stress. "You're as worried as I am, and you just don't want to admit it."

"And that's all part of being a leader. Anyway, you know we had times where we couldn't field a whole team back when you were a player. It's a cycle that goes on and on."

I sat down in the chair opposite him and ran a hand through my hair. I'd always kept it cropped short, army style, but I'd gone few weeks without a cut and it was proving very useful to grab when I was stressed. "I know, Rhod. I just want to make this team a success. I can't fuck anything else up."

"Still not talking to your young man then? I heard from a couple of the players that you seemed very cosy at the open training session."

I could feel my ears heating. "No, no, we're fine...well, there is this one thing. He's meeting his ex today."

"And you're worried they could rekindle something?"

"God, no. I'm worried he'll get hurt. And Nathan deserves not to be hurt. He deserves everything."

"I really need to meet this young man of yours. Did you apologise for your stupidly timed proposal?" Rhod smiled.

"He...agreed," I said.

"Well, isn't that romantic?" Rhod laughed.

There was a knock at the office door, and Ben stuck his head through. "Coach...uh...coaches, there are only eighteen of us in there, and I really don't know what we're gonna do."

"We'll be with you in just a moment," Rhod said. Ben nodded and left. The door closed behind him. I had no idea how Rhod always managed other people so implicitly; like he could tell people to leave a room without ever using the words. Everyone respected Rhod.

"Remember...remember how I said I'd employed you as long as you were a good influence to the lads?" Rhod asked. I nodded. "I need you to completely fucking disregard what I said."

"What?" I asked.

"When you were seventeen years old and we only had fifteen players up to play, that changing room was like a graveyard. The boys would think they were about to lose no matter how well they played. And there was one cocky big bastard who knew how to get everyone's mood up." Rhod pointed at me. "You'd say something stupid or pull out a bottle of some alcohol from God knows where, or sing a silly song, and the lads would just get *energised*. Right now I need stupid Finn to go in there and get a smile on their faces. I'm going to go in there now, and I need you to follow me in. Whatever I'm saying, no matter how inspiring it sounds, I don't care. Just do your thing."

Rhod stood with a groan and clapped me on the shoulder before he left the office. I looked down at my phone as it buzzed.

Nathan: Best of luck today. I'll try and make it down before the match starts. Pont is going to smash it x

Finn: Hope all goes OK 4 you today too. Let me know if you need anything, I'm here x

In all honesty I was more worried about Nathan meeting Lewis than I'd ever admit, but I'd promised him I would let him be a big boy and defend himself if he needed to. I just wished he hadn't given that bastard the time of day.

I scrolled through Spotify for an inspiring song for the lads. I could go with a classic, like *Eye of the Tiger*, or something stupid like *I Wanna Dance With Somebody* to get smiles on those faces. But I had an old Welsh rugby playlist I always used to play to myself the day of a Cardiff or Wales match. I just hoped the boys of today still knew who Max Boyce was.

I got the song ready to play, jumped up and down a bit before pushing open the door open and interrupting Rhod's speech at the same time I started the song playing.

"Dai works down the tower, in a pit called number four!" I shouted. Some of the boys looked very fucking confused, but Rhod's grin could have split his face in half as I spoke along with Max Boyce's live introduction to a legendary Welsh song. When I finally got to the chorus, more of the lads were smiling.

"Come on lads, fucking sing! " I shouted.

"And we were singing, hymns and arias, land of my fathers, ar hyd y nos!" most of them joined in, some of the younger lads still looked a bit confused, but by the third chorus were on their feet and singing along too.

"I don't care how many of us there are," I shouted. "I don't care what bastards they bring along. We are better, and bigger, and we can beat the shit out of Pandy on our worst day!"

The whole group of lads cheered. I checked my watch. "Right lads, let's get out on the field and beat the shit out of those fuckers!"

22

Chapter Twenty-Two - Nathan

I was tapping my ring absentmindedly on the side of a mug in the local church cafe as I waited for Lewis. It was weird, having an engagement ring on my finger, and I found myself playing with it constantly. But I didn't dislike it, not at all. And it was a good prop for the conversation I was ready to have today.

For a second, I let myself think about the man who'd given me the ring. And whether Finn's first full game in charge as a coach would be the roaring success he deserved. Because he deserved so much better than he got.

I heard the tinkle of the bell above the door and looked up as Lewis walked in. I gave him a very deliberate wave with my left hand, and his eyes didn't leave it as he walked towards me. It was like his eyes were glued to the ring on my finger.

In the light, I could tell that my impressions of him the night at the Pont Hotel were pretty accurate. He'd aged badly in the six years since I'd last seen him, with greying hair at his temples and a bit of a paunch coming on. It didn't bring me any pleasure to see him brought to this, but it didn't exactly hurt either.

Lewis sat down and for a few fragile seconds, neither of us said anything. Then when he did go to open his mouth, the kindly old waitress came to take his order. When she had brought him a cup of tea, he finally got his chance to speak.

"So I've been a bit of a shit," he said. I waited for him to carry on, but he didn't. He just lifted his mug with one shaking hand, and took a long slurp of his tea.

"Well, you got that right," I said. "So why meet now?"

"I just..." Lewis hesitated. "I don't know. I'm not here to beg for you back, if that's what you're thinking."

The thought had crossed my mind. "Well I'm glad. I said no six years ago. I'm not about to change my mind."

"Good. You deserve better. You have better." Lewis took anther sip whilst I tried to collect my jaw off the floor.

"What?" I finally managed.

"You deserve better than me, and you've obviously gotten it. I treated you like shit in high school, I strung you along, and I...I know now, some of the things I did wrong. I know that I wasn't...considerate, I guess."

It was the understatement of the fucking century, but still not something I expected to hear passing Lewis' lips.

"...thanks," was all I could bring myself to say. I took another long drink. Was Lewis going to talk more, or was I expected to say something now? That I forgave him? *Did* I forgive him?

"I just wanted to ask. How do you get happy?" Lewis asked after a minute.

"Happy?"

"Yeah, happy. How do you get...like you?"

I laughed without much humour. "I was harassed out of my home town by my ex-boyfriend and his big scary hookup, lived in exile in a tiny village in the middle of fucking nowhere, only to come home to a father who's insistent on making my home

CHAPTER TWENTY-TWO - NATHAN

life a living hell, and I'm in some kind of relationship with a man that probably sees me as his sappy little liability."

"You're joking, right?" asked Lewis.

"Which part?" I took the mug of coffee in front of me and swigged down the dregs like I was finishing a pint of beer.

"You're, like...yes, I was a stupid twat. So on your first point, you're right. But I had no idea Charlie was harassing you too. I haven't spoken to him in five fucking years. That's...that's not on."

"Seriously? He threatened me in my first couple of weeks back here. If I hadn't been with Finn..." I tailed off. Weirdly, looking back, that day just over a month before felt like a happy memory now. The fear I felt in this small town had faded. But I still remembered that he was such a big part of the reason I'd left so long ago. "Did he ever come out?"

Lewis looked around conspiratorially. "No. We didn't hook up after...after that one time."

"And have you..." I left the question open ended, and to be honest I didn't know exactly what I was asking. I hoped he'd fill in the blanks.

"I've not...been with anyone, since," admitted Lewis. "I think I always knew I was...I was going wrong with you, and I can only say how fucking sorry I am for being such a shit. And then that time with Charlie, he made me feel exactly like how I must have made you feel. Like a toy, or a tool to be used. So I did a bit of research. Not porn, I googled 'how to have gay sex'. Can you fucking believe that? And then I got led onto this video about cups of tea..."

I laughed. I was surprised by how easy this conversation with Lewis was. How much he'd grown. "I've only heard of that one recently. It was an eye opener."

"Fucking crazy, man. Anyway, by the time I'd figured out what I wanted, how to be me, how to be fucking proud of being... a queer, I guess, I was getting grey, getting fat and the cigarettes had wrecked my fucking teeth. I've tried Grindr, and other than sixty year olds wanting to shit on my chest I am not a fucking catch."

I was glad I had finished my coffee, because I would have snorted it all out of my nose at that one. "Jesus Christ, Lewis."

"Anyway, back to your points," he said. "Yeah, it was shit — what I did to you, what Charlie did to you — but you got the fuck out of here. Don't you know how many of us wish we'd done the same? You lived in Cardiff and then on the Welsh coast, and I live three streets away from the house where I grew up. I still see my shitty father every day because we work for the same fucking company. You *got out*, and I can apologise every fucking day for being the one who forced you out, but you did."

I sat in stunned silence, and Lewis seemed to take it as a sign to carry on. "And your dad is making your life a living hell? That's been my whole fucking life, and God knows your father has his reasons for being a prick. The rest of us just had shitty dads from birth. So big whoop. And you falling for a man who doesn't look at you twice? I was within three feet of you the other day and I think if I'd taken a step closer he'd have ripped my head off for getting too close. That man is as in love with you as anyone I've ever seen. So I'll ask you again. How do I get to be happy?"

"I told you, I'm not..." I paused. "I'm...fuck, I'm happy, aren't I?" And despite all the shit in my life, there was one thing. One person, who'd been the catalyst for it all. And we'd been dancing around each other like two idiots. Finn had made me happy. But did I make him happy? The thought of his big thigh pressed against mine. His dopey smile, and silly jokes. The way his face relaxed into blissed out ecstasy as I slid into him...

Fuck. My head was spinning. Of *course* Finn looked at me the same way I looked at him. Of *fucking* course. And here I was, wasting time in a quasi-therapy session with my ex.

"Sorry Lew, that's going to have to wait. I've got places to be. But I promise. I will carry on this conversation. I owe you that. But when it comes to being happy? I think I've got to go and grab happiness by the balls." I stood up, grabbed my coat and headed for the door. It wasn't until I was halfway to Pontycae's rugby ground that I realised I hadn't paid. *Fuck it.* Lewis could have that one little extra bit of penance.

Chapter Twenty-Three - Finn

The game was close. Too close, considering the massive skill gap we should have had between the two teams. But we had eighteen players altogether and Pandy had already injured three players. So at the very start of the second half, we had the fifteen players on the pitch and no more substitutes for injury. Our supporters were cheering from the sidelines — turnout was always good for a Pont-Pandy match, but the game was one that made me want to tear my hair out. I looked at Rhod's bald head and realised for the first time it might not be a genetic thing.

"Play a careful game, boys," I'd said during the half-time huddle. "We're five points up, all we need to do is maintain that. Don't risk injury, don't make any stupid tackles. Just play like your mother is watching, and defend as one."

Now, I was watching as the boys played carefully. Too carefully. Pandy were dangerously close to a try and our players were trying to keep themselves safe from the crush of bodies. "Push back!" I shouted. "Push it fucking back!"

I watched as one of their biggest players broke free of the pack

CHAPTER TWENTY-THREE - FINN

with his ball in hand and our lock ran straight at him. It would have been a spectacular tackle if their player hadn't sidestepped awkwardly. The two collided with a crack that could be heard from across the pitch.

"Fuck," I muttered.

"Exactly," Rhod replied. Our team physio ran across the pitch to check on the players. "Come on, get up, get up," I chanted under my breath. But after a minute the physio and a couple of players were helping both of the lads off the pitch. Pandy had a substitute to send on, but we would be down to fourteen men for the rest of the match. I wanted to scream, I wanted to have a right old temper tantrum right there on the sidelines. But I wasn't some playboy rugby player now, I was these lads' coach. They needed me to be there to provide encouragement, to keep up that inspiration for them even when things were going wrong.

The ref spoke to each of our captains before play carried on, but with fourteen players on the pitch it was pretty easy for Pandy to get a try past us. And then another, two minutes later.

"For fuck's sake!" Rhod muttered, hands shaking on the clipboard he always carried around with him. "We've not lost to Pandy in ten years and I don't plan on it today...go and get your kit on."

"What?"

"You heard me, go and find a kit big enough, grab some boots from the lost and found and get the fuck onto the pitch."

I ran behind the spectators, around the pitch to our changing rooms like my arse was on fire. I hadn't played rugby since... well, since all the shit had gone down. But it was time to give it a go again. Sure, it was probably cheating to have an ex-Welsh international on the pitch. But I was out of shape, and I wasn't about to let anything get between me and holding the ball again.

I grabbed the nearest XXL shirt and shorts, grabbed some socks and a muddy, smelly old pair of size thirteens. *Which gross bastard left these behind?* I wondered before reading the name tag inside. *Oh. Finn.* These were my old boots from my school days, and when I slipped my feet into them it was like coming home. If home was a muddy boot that had probably been used by forty different players since I had last played for Pont.

I ran out of the changing rooms, and as soon as there was a break in the play I ran through the spectators and on to the pitch.

The ref immediately ran up to me. "You can't be here, mate. The game is an amateur..."

"Call the rugby union. Check my status," I said before he could carry on. "I'm unaffiliated with any team. No-one wants me. So I'm allowed here."

Muttering, the ref walked away from me and I took my position in the line as he whistled to resume play. Pandy had possession of the ball and they were playing fast, dirty rugby. Ben was like gazelle as he chased them across the pitch and our team were in-sync, but somehow Pandy just had an edge. One familiar big bastard ran toward me with the ball and I took him down with ease. It was a fucking delight to be in the game like this again. I was so elated with tackling that I had completely forgotten that the game moved on straight afterwards, and missed my chance to tackle the next player or rip the ball from them. Luckily, with fifteen players again, we were playing in sync and one off ours managed to rip the ball and kick it out, into the other team's twenty-two. It rolled out of bounds

"Good one, mate!" I clapped our player — Ioan — on the

shoulder and he smiled at me. His risky manoeuvre had put us on the front foot a little bit, because the ball bouncing out in that spot - within 22 metres of the opposition try line — meant that we got the line-out. And line-outs were where I shone. I may not have played rugby in months, but I had designed our plays. And I was standing in for our downed lock, which was my preferred position anyway.

Ben stood on the sidelines ready to throw in the ball. "Right lads, gold one two!" Everyone took their positions and as Ben threw I jumped, two other players getting a death grip on my thighs to hold me higher for longer. The opposition player wasn't quite as tall as me and Ben had thrown beautifully, so I managed to get hold of the ball and I threw it backward down the line as soon as I was on the ground. It sailed through the air between players until one of our wingers got a beautiful corner try.

We all got the chance to catch our breath as our kicker lined up his next shot, and I noticed a couple of additions to our audience. Garrett and Bernie were stood next to Rhod, as well as Pete Grainger, Cardiff's new manager and Garrett's replacement as Garrett had moved on to coaching the Wales squad. Pete was an old legend in the English game. He was stood next to a player who'd joined Cardiff in my absence, George something-or-other.

But it wasn't the rugby royalty in the crowd that drew my attention. It was the flash of shocking pink and tortoiseshell spectacles. I waved over at Nathan with a grin, and he waved back just as enthusiastically. I was glad to see him so happy. Perhaps my worries about his meeting with Lewis had been for nothing. As our kicker sailed the ball between opposition posts and the crowd cheered, Nathan's gaze slid over to the opposing team. I noticed that the lad who I'd tackled earlier was staring at him with malice. *Oh.* I was so stupid. That was Lewis' friend, the one who'd terrorised Nathan in the pub before. If he went down a couple more times, perhaps that wouldn't be the worst thing in the world.

As we walked back to our half of the pitch to kick off again, I rallied the boys around me. "Win or lose, that's the energy, the power, the unity I want to see in you all. You're playing fucking fantastically, lads!"

"Another punt in the swear jar?" joked Ben. "Or just a *Don't say fuck every sentence* challenge."

"Fuck off," I shouted, giving him the two-fingered salute to drive my point home even further. He just laughed. *Kids. No respect these days.* Once he was done laughing at me, I pulled him aside.

"Do you know that big fucker on their team?" I asked quietly.

"Charlie? He's a bit of a bastard around town. Why?"

"Gonna teach the big bastard a lesson," I replied, gesturing for the whole team to get ready for Pandy's attack.

Pandy kicked the ball into our half and we pushed against them hard until we were all sweating and grimy in the August heat. But a bad rip meant that we had to go into a scrum. I walked towards the lads gathering to take my place, and I passed Charlie as I did. Subtly, he pulled at the bottom of my shirt to turn me around.

"Still fucking that little shit then?" he asked quietly. "Just know if he runs his mouth you won't always be around to protect him."

"Wanna bet?" I asked, taking my place in the scrum. Charlie was at the other side and I couldn't make direct contact with him, but I was raging. How dare anyone ever threaten Nathan?

CHAPTER TWENTY-THREE - FINN

How fucking dare he talk about him like that?

And then it was like everything clicked together. Charlie wasn't just defending lewis, that had never been it. He was scared for himself.

Nathan had *told* me without telling me, and only in that moment was I actually figuring it all out and putting the puzzle pieces together. Charlie was the piece of shit who'd run Nathan out of town because he'd been caught with Lewis. Charlie was one of those things that kept Nathan from his home out of fear. And I was fucking livid.

The Pandy player rolled the ball in at and angle and even with the best fight in us we weren't able to get the ball from them, so as it got passed out to their players running behind we got into a defensive line to take down any Pandy player that tried to get through.

I watched as Ben took the first hit, and he managed to stop a guy twice his weight from breaching the line. The ball was passed backwards along the line and we kept pace as a team, constantly calling out to one another and holding the line back. I was so proud of the lads for holding out defensively. We could never have expected so many of these boys to play a full eighty minute game, but we were nearing the end of it and despite the points we were down by we were losing well, and with dignity.

One of Pandy's players passed backward to the big bastard in front of me. Charlie. The second we locked eyes, he had the decency to look fucking terrified before I ran at him, and took him down.

In that moment, I didn't care about the game. I didn't care about the points. I just wanted that man to know he couldn't hurt Nathan ever again. Because no one got in between me and the man I loved.

The man I loved.

I.

Loved.

It was obvious, then, as the world slowed down and both Charlie and I crashed to the floor. As the ball rolled forward out of his hands and the ref blew his whistle to declare an advantage to our team. An advantage our kicker took by kicking the ball out of play, and the ref blew the whistle to signal the end of play. It was so blindingly obvious that I was deeply in love with Nathan, and that the pretence that we were pretending was the real...pretence. *Yeah, I'm still no poet.* So I stood up and crossed the field to that man at the sidelines, ignoring the cheers from the Pandy supporters and gentle *tuts* from the Pont ones. Charlie was having trouble getting up, but I didn't care. That was for the medics to sort, and he only had himself to blame.

I didn't care.

Because Nathan was there at the sidelines and looking at me, and I was looking at him, and I could only hope in that moment that the look he was giving me reflected what was in my eyes and in my mind.

As soon as I was close, I said it. "I love you. And that's real. That's me saying it honestly, without the expectation that you'll say it back. You know I won't push you beyond what you're comfortable with-"

"I love you too, you big idiot," Nathan replied.

"Oh," was all I could think to reply.

"Is now the time?" Rhod butted in from the side.

"Yes," I said.

"Probably not," said Nathan at the same time. "Go on, go bolster the team. I'll be here when you get back. I'll always be here when you get back."

CHAPTER TWENTY-THREE - FINN

I felt fucking giddy as I jogged back over to my slightly dejected-looking team and called them into a circle around me. "C'mon boys, you played well. There were fourteen of you at one point, and you held your own. Hell, some of you have never even played a full eighty minutes before. So we're going to go into that clubhouse with our heads held high, and we're gonna be gracious losers to Pandy. Because though we don't deserve to lose, they certainly deserved that win. And I'll make sure Rhod puts his hand in his pocket for beers for every single one of you. Now go and shower, you muddy buggers."

They all cheered and ran across the field to the showers. Even with my speech, I didn't want to go and celebrate myself. I wanted to be with Nathan, and if Charlie was going to be there I wasn't going to make Nathan stay anywhere uncomfortable.

So when I turned around, I was shocked to see Nathan stood on one side of the field with Charlie. From the distance I couldn't see if Charlie looked like he was ready to knock Nathan out so I ran over. I was determined to protect Nathan to the ends of the Earth.

As it turned out, I didn't need to bother. As I got close enough to listen, Nathan held one hand up to stop me. "My fight, Finn," he said. "I've dealt with one of my problems today. Now it's time to deal with another."

Close up, I could see that Charlie's face was grey and he was holding on to the small of his back. Maybe I had done some damage on the rugby pitch. Nathan looked up at him, and spoke with authority like I'd heard when he faced up to the men in Cardiff. "I don't care what you think of me, Charlie. All I see is a scared little man in the body of an ogre trying his best to do damage control. I have no intention of outing you, and I never did. So you need to take a long, hard look in the mirror and decide if you want to carry on living a lie. But I will not be your punching bag. I'm sticking around, and you can either get used to that or you can be the one to fuck off out of this little village this time. Am I clear?"

"Clear," said Charlie quietly.

"And if you don't listen to reason, my fiancé here is willing to get a few more hits in on you to drive home the lesson. And to be honest, I wouldn't mind getting a few punches in whilst he holds your hands back."

Charlie looked between us both with no colour left in his face, and turned to walk away. "Hey!" Nathan shouted. "I'm still after an apology. Lewis managed one today, so I'm sure you can stretch to it too."

"…sorry. I'm…I'm really sorry," Charlie muttered. And then he was walking away, not toward the changing rooms, but back toward the village.

"Did that feel good?" I asked Nathan, holding my arms open to him.

"Really fucking good," he admitted, wrapping his arms around my waist and laying his head on my chest. "Almost as good as watching you in your element, playing rugby."

"It felt…good," I admitted. "But not as good as I remembered. I think rugby brings out the parts of me I don't always love. I could have really hurt Charlie there."

"Shame, Garrett was on the sidelines singing your praises." Nathan said. I felt my cheeks heat. It was nice to be noticed again. "And I don't mind you teaching him a lesson or two."

"What a wonderful fake fiancé you have, he's so violent," I replied.

It took Nathan a second. "Did you just paraphrase Tom Baker's Doctor Who at me?"

"Maybe, young Padawan. Now let me get fully showered off so we can go and live long and prosper."

"Anything but *Trek*," Nathan complained, but he was smiling. "And I don't know how fake this any more."

"Nor me," I said. "I love you. I know it's stupidly early, I know our whole relationship has been under false pretences. But I can't pretend that I'm pretending any more. I've never felt such a connection with anyone."

"Me neither," said Nathan. "You make me feel safe."

"Shall we go and celebrate?" I asked. "Come meet more of the rugby lads. Everyone at the open day loved you and Ben is collecting older queer role models like Pokémon cards. And I want to chat to Garrett about why the fuck he's here."

"Sounds good to me, I shouldn't need to be home until…" he looked down at his phone. "Shit, I've got like twelve missed calls from Dad." He held the phone up to his ear, and frowned. "He's not answering. I've…I'll have to go home, check on him."

"I'll come with you,'" I said.

"No, don't worry about it. It shouldn't take too long, and you should be celebrating."

"If you want me there, I'm there," I said. I held out a hand and Nathan took it. "Let's go."

24

Chapter Twenty-Four - Nathan

Having Finn by my side and knowing that he was a more permanent addition there now — not that we'd spoken about permanence, but surely *I love you* was more than a temporary thing — just felt so easy.

Being with Finn had started as a shield for me to protect myself from bullies. But our relationship had evolved, and now more than anything he felt like a comfort blanket. I could protect myself, but he was there to keep me warm and content and I hoped he felt the same about me.

His metal-studded boots *clip-clipped* on the pavement as he walked alongside me and I looked him up and down. Finn was muddy and grazed from rugby. "Shit, sorry, I should have sent you to shower off," I said.

"Don't be stupid. We need to get home for your dad."

"If he's not just struggling with the fucking TV remote again," I said. "I've had enough of him being deliberately pathetic. If he's gonna be the third man I have to give a bollocking to today..."

"Who was the first?" Finn asked.

CHAPTER TWENTY-FOUR - NATHAN

Oh. Shit. We hadn't actually talked about that yet. "Lewis."

"Shit! I totally forgot? Did he..."

"Try it on with me? No," I laughed. "He actually asked me how I got so happy, and how I got you all lovestruck. Made me realise that he was very right. I was punishing myself by acting like we were pretending. So I ran off, left him with the bill and came to tell you I loved you."

"Fucking hell," said Finn.

"Quite."

We walked up the street to my house. The living room curtains were still drawn, and I couldn't see any lights on. "That's not right," I muttered. "He leaves every light on in the house just to piss my mum off about the electric bill..."

I hurried quicker toward the front door and Finn kept pace, never letting go of my hand.

I opened the door and peered into the darkness of the hallway. "Dad?" I called.

I couldn't hear a reply. "Dad? You there?"

Still nothing. I crept into the house, turning on the light as I went. Finn followed silently.

"Dad?" I called. Then I heard the groan coming from the direction of the kitchen. I ran into the kitchen, but it was as dark as the rest of the house. The light in the hallway off the kitchen was on, and I could hear running water. "Shit," I said. I walked down the hallway, not even conscious if Finn was walking behind me or not any more. The shower in the shower room was running and the door was closed. I tried the handle. "Dad, you in there?" I asked.

"Nathan," I heard him reply, so quietly. But nothing else. I yanked at the door again. It still wouldn't budge. "Shit, shit, shit!" I pulled at the handle until my knuckles turned white.

"Dad, can you reach the door? Have you locked it?"

"Budge over," Finn whispered to me, using his big paws to move me gently out of the way. "Are you particularly attached to this door?" he asked. Without waiting for a reply, he took a step back and then shoulder-barged it. It moved but didn't open. "Ow," said Finn. "Let's try that again." He took two steps back and barged at the door. This time it buckled inward, taking some of the door frame with it. Warm steam billowed out of the room and I ran past Finn into there, almost slipping on the tiled floor.

Which it appeared my father had done. He was laying propped up against the wall and just out of the flow of the overhead shower. He was completely naked, and his wheelchair was turned over in the far dry corner of the bathroom. "Oh, Dad..." I muttered. "Finn. Call an ambulance." I didn't wait for his response, I knew he'd do it for me.

I shut off the shower and grabbed a towel to preserve my Dad's dignity. "Dad, you with me?" I asked. His eyes were open, at least. He didn't seem to be bleeding anywhere and both his full leg and his stump were resting on the cold tiles.

"Dad, you here with me?" I asked.

"Slipped and fell," he muttered. "Was just trying...to do things myself."

"Was this really the time to figure out independence?" I half joked.

"S'pose not..." he muttered. I checked his pulse, which seemed to be fine.

"Did you hit your head?" I asked.

"No. M'arm hurts though..."

"OK, Dad. I'm going to try and get you into your chair. Do you think you can help me?" He seemed groggy, but if he hadn't hit

CHAPTER TWENTY-FOUR - NATHAN

his head it was probably exhaustion or hypothermia. I needed him dry and clothed.

"Ambulance in ten minutes," said Finn.

"Thank God," I said. I used the towel to dry my Dad off as quickly and with as much dignity as I could. I could see a big bruise forming on his left arm so I was as gentle as I could be. "Finn, can you help me with his shirt?" I asked.

"Who's this?" Dad muttered as Finn lifted his good arm to get it through his t-shirt sleeve.

"Dad, Finn, Finn, Dad. I'm glad you could meet each other. Now let's get your pants on. Finn, lift please?"

With more strength than I possessed, Finn lifted my Dad by his underarms so I could shuffle his trousers on under his thighs. "Well done, Dad. You're doing so well. Now we're going to help you to your wheelchair, OK? Let us know if anything hurts too much and we'll stop."

"Thanks. Nathan. Always a good lad..." Dad muttered.

"Oh God, Finn, he really is delirious." I grabbed under his bad arm and Finn grabbed under his good one, and with some weight on his single leg Dad managed to help us somewhat in manoeuvring him over to his wheelchair. When we sat him down, he sighed.

"Not delirious," Dad muttered. "I've just been a wanker."

"That we can agree on, but we can talk about this later. All I care about is you being well," I said. I wheeled him out of the bathroom and into the kitchen. "Do you need water?"

"Please," he said. I grabbed a plastic cup and filled it up from the sink.

"Here you go, drink." I supported the cup with one hand in case he dropped it but he held it firm as he drank.

"Coming back to us?" I asked. He shivered but looked up to

177

me with clear eyes.

"Never left," he said quietly. "Well, that's a lie. I completely bloody checked out. But I heard my son talking about me being a right wanker a couple of days ago and decided it was time to come back to the real world."

"You heard all that?" I asked. Dad just nodded.

"Do you want me to leave?" Finn asked.

"No," both Dad and I said at the same time. The force in Dad's voice surprised me.

"Stay here," Dad said. "I need a witness."

"I'm not going to smother you," I muttered. He barked out a laugh.

"I wouldn't blame you if you did. I've been more trouble than I'm worth." Dad said ruefully, and finished off his water. "But...I thought I'd get more independent. Told your mother not to bother helping me shower this morning. And look where that got me."

"I was talking more like getting your own beer from the fridge, Dad," I said. "We can work our way up to showering when you have the faintest idea how to use the shower seat."

"Just...sorry," Dad said. "I didn't want to help myself, but I resented your help too. And I didn't want you back in this place where you were caused so much pain. So I tried pushing you away."

"Well, shit happens, Dad," I said. "But thing is, you were the one person I could rely on as a kid to support me. When I was stupid enough to dye my hair every colour under the sun in school you were there for me. When I was with Lewis and getting caught in the rugby club toilets with him, you were the one who made sure I didn't get a bloody criminal record. You supported me through everything, no matter how much

CHAPTER TWENTY-FOUR - NATHAN

of an idiot I was or how I pushed you away. So I want to help you. Meet me halfway and I'll do anything to pay you back for how fantastic a father you were to me. I'd push this fucking wheelchair up Everest for you."

A tear leaked down Dad's cheek. "Everest it is then."

The front door opened and Mum stepped through. "Is everything OK? I had missed calls from you and I couldn't get hold of- Oh, hi Nathan. Hi Finn."

Blue flickering lights filled the room, and there was no time for pleasantries as I wheeled Dad out of the door and to the waiting ambulance. He might seem fine, but I wanted to know that he was, and that he hadn't sustained any internal injuries in his fall.

"He fell in the shower," I explained to Mum as a couple of paramedics got out.

"Right, let me go with him to the hospital," she said. "You've done your bit for the night."

In minutes, they had Dad bundled up in the ambulance with Mum holding his hand. The ambulance pulled out into the street, and Finn and I were left standing in the warm September night. And I wrapped my arms around his big frame and held him tight.

"You OK?" he asked.

"I will be," I said.

"Want to come back to mine this evening? I don't like the thought of you alone in the house for hours after everything you've been through.'

"Yes please," I said almost as soon as he'd gotten the sentence out.

Finn patted his shorts, groaned and held up one tiny key. "All my stuff is in the changing rooms. Including my house key. So we'll have to stop off at the rugby pitch again."

"Awesome." I laced my fingers through his, and we walked back down the street toward Pont's rugby grounds.

* * *

We walked into the darkened gym, and Finn raised his arm to sniff. "Jesus," he said. "I forgot how rugby can make a man *smell*."

"Like a man," I said under my breath. All I could smell on him was freshly cut grass and an earthy smell and I really liked it. Finn locked the door behind us. In the darkness, I reached out one hand to grab his.

We walked past the gym equipment and Finn and Rhod's office and headed into the shower room. Finn flicked the light switch on. His bag was stuffed into a corner and his clothes were hanging out of it. "Got changed in a rush," he explained.

"I saw you run on," I replied.

And then for a few seconds we stood there. Three feet apart. The whole world at our feet under a couple of inches of old tile. And I didn't know what to do. Or say. Because there was a tension between us now we knew we were real.

And then Finn was stepping in closer to me and I was moving to meet him, and those big hands were touching my face, tilting my lips up as he leaned down to kiss me.

God, I was safe in his hands. And not just safe, but loved. And as our tongues danced around one another and I rubbed at Finn's massive shaft through his thin rugby shorts, I knew there was nowhere else I wanted to be.

Finn broke off the kiss. "Is all of this OK with you?"

CHAPTER TWENTY-FOUR - NATHAN

I appreciated him asking. It made me feel even more safe, and somehow even more turned on. "From this moment onward, Finn Roberts, I promise you I'm comfortable enough to say no if I don't want something."

"I know, but enthusiastic consent is good," he said.

I grabbed at his thick bulge through his shorts and gave a tug that made him moan. "Enthusiastic enough?"

"Yup, all...all good with me," Finn breathed as I dipped my hand into those shorts to pull out his length. I loved how warm and weight his cock felt in my hand.

"Actually..." Finn said, and I took an immediate step back. There was hesitation in that voice, and I knew what it was like to have my boundaries crossed, so the last thing I wanted to do was to disrespect his. "...I just want a shower before we start doing stuff properly. My junk is all sweaty and gross."

He stripped off his boots, shirt and shorts with no hesitation and headed toward the shower. I followed just behind, still fully clothed. He was still hard and I wanted my hands on him as soon as he'd let me. Finn turned on the shower, dipped one hand in and splashed cold water all over me.

"You bastard!" I said.

"You should get out of those wet clothes," he said, stepping under the shower.

"I'm going to stay in them now just to spite you," I replied as Finn started to wash away all the mud and grime from the day. "Need help washing?"

"I could always use a pair of fucking good hands," Finn said.

I took off my glasses, placed them carefully on the floor and stepped forward until I was close to him. I could feel droplets of water landing on my t-shirt and exposed skin as I reached for his cock again.

"I want to taste you," I said.

Finn leaned down and captured my mouth in his again. "Do I taste good enough?" he asked between kisses, moving his mouth from mine and to my cheek, and then my neck.

"I want to taste your cock," I whispered. The water that was cascading down Finn's back, through his hair and neck was starting to soak through my t-shirt but I'd told him I wasn't going to take my clothes off just to spite him.

"Taste it, then." Finn commanded.

I lowered myself to my knees on the tile floor. I released my own cock from my shorts as I took the head of his in my mouth. I loved the taste of him on my tongue, and I coaxed out pre-cum from the tip. I thought I must look ridiculous kneeling on the floor with my clothes soaked through but Finn's groans were like music to my ears and the warm water now dripping on to my shoulders made the whole experience even more sensual. I used my left hand to steady myself against the wall as I took more of his cock into my mouth and used my right to wank myself.

I worked my way onto Finn's cock slowly. I had never been very good at deep-throating and especially with Finn's monster cock it was going to be difficult. But every groan and whimper I managed to get out of him made me want to take him deeper, made me want to please him.

I pulled off his cock for a second. "Face fuck me, Finn," I said.

"Sure?" he asked.

"Now," I said, dipping my mouth back onto his cock-head. I moved my left hand from the wall to his furry arse cheek to pull him in, and I gripped on to it as he started to thrust — gently at first — into my mouth.

"Fuck," said Finn, starting to move faster and deeper. When

CHAPTER TWENTY-FOUR - NATHAN

I gagged, I kept a grip on his arse to keep him going. My cock was twitching in my hand with every thrust into my throat. I was so close to finishing and all I wanted was for him to—

"Fuck, Nath, I'm close." Finn said. It was a warning to move away if I wanted to. But I didn't want to. I kept a grip on his arse as he thrust harder, faster, and then his knees were shaking as his cock jerked in my mouth and coated my tongue with his release. I gagged but swallowed as he kept pumping that release into my mouth, and then my orgasm came crashing through and I came all over the tiled floor between his feet.

Finn offered me a hand and I took it, my legs shaking as I tucked myself away into my wet shorts. He kissed me gently and I tangled my fingers through his coarse chest hair.

"I was going to suggest celebrating with the boys if they're still out but..." Finn gestured at my soaked clothing. "I guess that's not really an option."

"Home, cuppa, nudity, *Thrones of Blood*?" I suggested. " And hope no one sees us walking home and asks why I look like I've been stood out in the rain."

"Sounds like my kind of night, real boyfriend." Finn kissed me again and shut off the spray with one hand. He pulled on boxers over his wet legs and smiled at me. And I knew I wanted to do this over and over again, for as long as he'd have me. Finn was mine and I was his, and there was nothing fake about it.

25

Chapter Twenty-Five - Finn

"Are you sure you can do this?" I asked Noel for what must've been the thousandth time because he groaned at the same time as Nathan.

"I can fucking do it," he said. "It might be tough, but I'm made of stronger stuff than that now."

He looked up at Nathan with such love in his eyes that it was hard to believe he'd ever been a right bastard to live with. But I knew it might take some time for Nathan to come round to this sudden change in attitude.

"Pete should be meeting us here," I said. "Nice of him to invite us on a family hike but I've no idea why..."

I went round to the back of the car and grabbed Noel's wheelchair. Together with Nathan I helped manoeuvre him from the seat into the wheelchair.

"When I said I'd help you up Everest, Dad, I did not realise you intended it to be so soon."

"It's hardly *Everest*," said Noel. He pointed up at the top of the hill. "It's grassy all the way to the top, it can't be that high."

"Whatever you say," Nathan countered. "I'm still going to

CHAPTER TWENTY-FIVE - FINN

be asking the big man to do most of the pushing."

"Watch who you're calling big," I shot back. I scanned the car park at the base of the hill, but no one had turned up yet. And then I saw the familiar coach coming over the horizon.

"Oh for fucks sake," I muttered. Nathan followed my eyeline and grinned. "I feel I've been invited under false pretences."

"What, because your ex-coach has invited the entirety of the Cardiff Old Navy squad to a friendly hike? I can't imagine why..."

The bus stopped and about twenty lads piled out, all led by Pete Grainger, Cardiff's newest head coach. He smiled as he approached and held out a hand to shake, and then shook both Nathan and Noel's hands too. "Ready for a climb, boys?"

"I had no idea you were bringing the whole Cardiff team," I said. "When you asked me, you said it was a family trip you were inviting us on."

"This team are the closest thing I've got to a family," said Pete. "I wasn't lying."

"Sure..." I said. I watched as the last stragglers got off the bus, followed by Garrett and Bernie. "And those two?"

"These two just wanted a nice bus trip, right babe?" Bernie said, looking at Garrett.

Babe? There was definitely something going on with them. But with my own...weird start to a relationship with Nathan, I didn't want to pry. I looked down at the ring on Nathan's hand where it rested on the back of Noel's wheelchair. I was waiting for him to ask me about what we did with the engagement ring now. I didn't want him to, though. I liked looking at that ring where it sat.

"Ready to climb a mountain?" Garrett asked.

I smiled. "Noel is helping me get some strength training in,

I'll be pushing him most of the way up."

"Nonsense. Lads!" Garrett called over to two of the boys. "Help this wonderful gentleman up the hill, will you?"

Two of the bigger rugby lads ran over and held out hands for a high-five from Noel. Within seconds, they were whisking him away from us. Bernie made a beeline for Nathan and grabbed him by the left arm. Suddenly I was in between Garrett and Pete at the rear of the pack and I realised I'd been swindled into a conversation I wasn't sure I was ready to have.

"This better not be another intervention," I said. "Because if you wanted to do that you should've invited Rhys and Callum. They're experts now."

"Not quite," laughed Pete. We walked up the hill in silence for a couple of minutes. It was a warm day and my brow was getting moist, but it wasn't all that exerting. And somehow, I could see the two lads who'd taken responsibility for Noel leading the pack ahead. Somewhere in the middle of all the rowdy rugby players was Nathan, pink hair flashing in the sun. I couldn't imagine him being so comfortable in amongst all of that just a couple of months ago, but he always seemed at ease around Bernie.

"Are you happy, Finn?" asked Garrett after another few minutes.

"You know what? For the first time in a while, I really am," I said. "I'm enjoying my job that pays me peanuts, I have a wonderful..." I hesitated, "...Nathan. And I'm feeling for the first time ever like I'm not playing to someone else's fiddle."

"Ah. Great." Pete said from my other side. He didn't sound totally thrilled that i was happy.

"What Pete means to say is, you're missed," said Garrett. "You needed your time off. We let you take it. But we know what

CHAPTER TWENTY-FIVE - FINN

we're missing."

"And we is…"

"Cardiff. And Wales. We want you back in the game." Pete was quick and to the point, and I appreciated it.

My whole world-view as to what was important had shifted in the space of a few weeks. But I still felt the echo of hurt in what I said next. "No."

"No?" asked Garrett. "What do you mean, *No*?"

"I mean…no," I said. "I spent so long running to get away from home and fucking hell, there's a big part of me that wants to get out in front of the crowds at the Millennium Stadium again. But I really fucking suffered out there on the field some days. And some days, it wasn't even suffering. Rugby made me feel so high I felt indestructible. And then I got home and I drank, or I fucked, or I did something destructive just to bring me back down to Earth. High or low, rugby *fucked me up*. And I've found something I enjoy now. I love coaching the boys. I love being an actual positive role model for the first time in my life, and I love coming home to Nathan and helping him pack figures from obscure Romanian sci-fi shows I can't even pronounce. So it makes the thought of going out onto the field, breaking myself every week and expecting that gorgeous man to fix me every single week difficult. I have put him through enough."

"Well that's good," said Garrett. "Because it makes the bigger part of our offer even easier to put to you. We've seen you coach and we've seen you play. I saw those lads on the field give you more respect than they give the ref. So maybe give some thought to the fact that we would like you to be a positive role model in Cardiff too. Come and learn from the coaching staff, get a formal coaching qualification with Cardiff. And if you want a few games to keep yourself sharp, no pressure. You can do that. But this deal is about us doing what we can for you and you doing what you want for us. And in time, if you're half the coach we think you are...well, neither of us is going to live forever."

I stopped, and both of them stopped with me. For a few seconds, I was just looking for that bright pink hair in amongst the crowd. I wanted to know my little fantasy man was close, to anchor me in reality. "I...need time to think," I said. "It sounds...fucking amazing, if I'm honest. But it's a lot. I need to talk to my...my Nathan."

"Well..." started Pete, but Garrett put a hand out to stop him I could see why Pete had brought Garrett along. Pete wasn't exactly diplomatic. Garrett hadn't been either, last time he'd coached me. But I sensed that something or someone had punctured that rough exterior.

"Take all the time you need," said Garrett. "We want you, and we can wait if that means having you fully on board."

"...thank you, really." I nodded at them both and doubled my walking speed. They were coaches, not athletes. Not any more. They wouldn't keep up.

I weaved through the group of lads until I spotted Nathan's pink hair again, and I called out to him to stop. The lads kept walking, and Nathan and Bernie slowed until I was level with them.

"Thanks for looking after my gorgeous...my Nathan, Bern," I said. "Can I steal him for a few minutes?"

"Sure, I'll just go back to my...to Garrett," he said. Nathan looked like he was doing his best not to laugh.

I waited until the rugby lads were far enough ahead, and checked the coaches and Bernie were still lagging behind, before

CHAPTER TWENTY-FIVE - FINN

I spoke.

"They've offered me a place," I said.

"On the team? Playing again?"

"Well...and coaching," I said.

"Wow..." Nathan said. I could tell he was wrestling with the question. "You going to take it?"

"I don't know," I admitted. "I need...not permission...what's the word?"

"Oversight? Advice? A kick up the arse?"

"Fuck it, permission was the word. I just didn't want people to think i was whipped. I need your permission."

"What *people?*" Nathan looked around, as if to emphasise how far we'd drifted from anyone else. "And you definitely don't need my permission to do anything."

"It's just...I want to be excited, Nath. I want to look forward to playing again, to helping push people like me to be better in rugby and better at life than I ever was. But I don't always like the pressure rugby puts on me. I don't want to be a burden on you if it all gets too much."

Nathan threaded his fingers through mine and pulled me to a stop. "Listen to me, Finn Roberts. I cannot promise to stop you making stupid decisions, or silly things. I cannot promise I will always be patient with you, or say the perfect thing, or know how to make you feel better when you're down. But I will be here. I will be here for as long as you need me and want me. Your problems are my privilege to bear."

"I love you," I said. I could feel tears welling up in my eyes. "So much."

"I know, I'm amazing," Nathan deadpanned. "But seriously, I love you too. You big lump. So if you want to take on the job, I am here for you. And I will tell you honestly if I think it's all getting too much."

I could feel the biggest grin stretching at my cheeks. I was going to be playing rugby again. And coaching. Around the lads, but with Nathan by my side. I could do anything. We started walking again. Having broached the toughest topic of all, the next monumental task felt so incredibly easy. I held his left hand up to my cheek and kissed the glinting gold ring that sat on it.

"I love you," I said. "And I know we agreed to be like, real boyfriends, but I've been thinking about how we solve this... fiance situation since I got us into it. And I think the best solution to the problem...is not to solve it."

"That made no fucking sense at all," said Nathan. "Oh fuck, I'm even swearing like you now."

"Stop fucking swearing, it's not fucking civilised," I joked.

"OK but seriously, what is the solution to this?" Nathan held up the ring so it was up closer to my face again."

"Marry me," I said. "I might not have proposed in the most... romantic way, but I know we're the real deal. I want to be with you forever and I hope you feel the same."

"So you want this fake engagement to get real?" Nathan asked.

"...if you'll have me," I said. I suddenly felt less confident. What if Nathan wasn't ready for this? What if he felt that we were moving too quickly? What if we-

"We've reached the peak, love," said Nathan. "You can stop walking now."

"Oh." I hadn't realised that we'd reached the summit of the mountain, and were now surrounded by Welsh rugby players. I felt gutted that Nathan couldn't answer the question now, not without revealing our whole ruse. Nathan kept hold of my

CHAPTER TWENTY-FIVE - FINN

hand and dragged me over to where his father sat, wheelchair covered in dust. But he was smiling at the beautiful view as one of the lads described a particularly gruesome tackle injury he'd once seen.

"Hey, Dad," Nathan cut in. "Finn and I were just talking dates for the wedding. What do you think, summer or winter? And how do you look in navy?"

And then he looked at me and winked. And I knew I was hooked forever.

* * *

A note from Matt...

Thank you for reading *Lord of the Lock!* It wasn't the most conventional book I've ever written, and it didn't fit a lot of the romance tropes so I've had some trouble figuring out its niche. It's the most personal book I've put out so far, and certain elements are ripped from life.

I hope you enjoyed reading Nathan and Finn's story as much as I enjoyed writing it. If you want to read more in the series, then you can read the story of how Rhys and Callum fell in love in *Pitch Prince*. And Garrett and Bernie's story is exclusive to my newsletter subscribers, so if you'd like to sign up to receive it for free head to my website at www.mattpetersauthor.com.

I'd like to thank Bella Lucas for her fantastic read-over and edit. It's a stronger piece of fiction because of Bella.

If you enjoyed, please leave a review. And I'm always open to talking with readers at my email address, matt@mattpetersauthor.com.

There's more to come in the Rucking Rugby Men Series, so keep your eyes peeled! I've got more small-town Pont drama as well as some steamy international rugby-football romance planned.

Thank you again for reading. Every read makes my little author dreams come true.

Other Books by Matt Peters

West Wales Romance
Handy Man
Hollywood Crush
Full Service
Also available as a trilogy box-set via Kindle

Rucking Rugby Men
Pitch Prince
Rugby Royal (Newsletter Bonus Serial)

Milton Keynes UK
Ingram Content Group UK Ltd.
UKHW011817240823
427440UK00004B/319